Surviving Mae West

Surviving Mae West

Priscilla A. Rodd

VANDALIA PRESS

MORGANTOWN 2006

Vandalia Press, Morgantown 26506

© 2005 by Priscilla A. Rodd and by West Virginia University Press

All rights reserved

Printed in the United States of America

13 12 11 10 09 08 07 06   10 9 8 7 6 5 4 3 2

ISBN 1-933202-07-6

Library of Congress Cataloging-in-Publication Data

Priscilla A. Rodd 1974 -
Surviving Mae West/Priscilla A. Rodd
viii, 208p. 23 cm.

Library of Congress Control Number: 2005937637

Vandalia Press is an imprint of West Virginia University Press

Cover image: "Self-portrait with Fingers, Eye and Ear" © 2001 Helen Payne
Book design by Than Saffel
Printed in USA by Bookmasters, Inc..

For my husband, Deane,
my lover, best friend, and colleague.
Life began anew when we met,
and I am forever grateful
to have you at my side.

And to my parents, Judy and Tom,
who demonstrated how to pursue a dream.
Your support and love have carried me.

Acknowledgments

Winston Fuller, for igniting the spark. Gail Adams, for her inspiration and too many lessons to name. Chuck Kinder, for his secret feminist heart and for always seeing the wild possibilities. Lewis "Buddy" Nordan, for the three-act structure and verb lessons. Mary Rodd Furbee, for early lessons on commas, for the philosophy that a hundred rejections is just the beginning, and for the belief that life only gets good after the age of twenty-three. Dr. Diane Trumbull, for teaching me about the importance of telling a person's story. The West Virginia University Press, for busting butt and taking a chance.

Deane Lindsey Kern, for the edits, the pep talks, the late nights, and the countless hours of support and help. Judy Rodd, who always encouraged us to "tell me a story" and who believed that 90 percent of education was reading books. Tom Rodd, for his appreciation of honesty and for his rebellious and artistic spirit. Grandma, for cheap rent and a love of literature. John Temple, for being a colleague and friend with inspiring ambition and skill. Helen Payne, for shared artistic ideas and the gorgeous cover painting. Montague Kern, for her enthusiasm and willingness to back me. And, finally, I thank the rest of my family and friends who enrich my life and my art.

October 1995

October 12

I wash off the makeup and glitter and study myself in the dressing room mirror. Through a film of hairspray, my breasts look like limp water balloons pinned up at a county fair. Sweaty strands of black hair cling to my shoulders. My rib cage strains like a breastplate beneath my skin, suspended from jutting collarbones.

I'm sitting at my kitchen table now, feeling too thin. That night, two weeks ago, I decided that if I didn't stop stripping, the stress of public exhibition would snap my bones and spill my guts over the slick stage. Imagine the catcalls.

So, tonight was my first shift at the brothel. On my way uptown in the cab, I quietly chanted the house number. The identical brownstones didn't confuse me like they did when I interviewed.

I should sleep, but I'm too wired. The morning vendors are unpacking paper lanterns and bags of slippers in the street below. I'm running my toes over Pandy's sleek fur, trying to relax.

I only saw one client. Whistling John. The guys choose their own code names, and he works as a jingle musician. Balding, with a beer belly, he's the generic, middle-aged man. But the Whistler grew soulful during his oral solo. I actually came.

Room 3 enhanced our encounter. A canopy bed, layered with a floral bedspread and pink sheets, crowds the room. A white loveseat presses into one corner, and sitting on the side table is a plastic bouquet that looks like wildflowers in the dim light.

I got nervous when John asked me to clarify a price—not part of the routine.

See, five to ten of us are corralled into the Living Room, and once we're picked out of the herd, we lead a guy to his room. Before briefly exiting, we tell him to get Completely Comfortable, which means he must take off all of his clothes, including his socks. Stripping entirely naked is supposedly against police protocol, so Diane requires sock removal as a final precaution.

Then, we pop back in and ask how long he's staying. Prompted on the phone about prices and routines, the guys hand us the money for an hour or a half hour. Either way, discussing money in the brothel is taboo.

Wide-eyed, I remembered the back-up plan. I told John to call Diane on the intercom (one in each room) if he was confused about anything.

No, he said, I'm pretty sure I'm right. Keep the change, in fact. Then he rolled onto the bed; his butt was as pink as an orangutan's.

It shocked me for that second, his nudity.

I don't know why he bucked protocol. He knows I'm new. Maybe he tested me for Diane. If so, I guess I passed.

We're taught to take the money without comment and excuse ourselves to hide the cash in a purse or our shoes or any safe place. The last step is to call down on the intercom to say we're in Room 3 or 4 for a half hour. Or an hour. Or whatever.

I assume he enjoyed himself, but truthfully his whole body and face blended into a mass of flesh I simply concentrated on stimulating. Rub this thigh, those biceps. Like a hot potato—you don't get a good look.

I'm told clients like eating us out. We're allowed to ask for a dental dam, and I suppose I should, but forcing guys to lick plastic?

Powdered latex? Blowjobs are much riskier, and we're required to roll out a condom long before our tongue touches a penis.

Personal-life wise, attacks still sneak up. Even as I'm writing, re-laxing, I'm shaking like I caught a chill. Nothing and nobody feels familiar. My face burns. Time to take a shower.

October 14

Susan returned from visiting her folks today and found me asleep, buck-naked on our black-and-white kitchen floor, one hand wrapped around a bag of M&M's. Very rock-star.

Knowing a bit about my attacks, she nudged me awake with her foot and handed me my robe and a cold beer. We both started to chuckle after a couple chugs, even though my breasts were sore from being smushed against the hard floor.

Sliding my Tammy Wynette CD into our stereo, Susan sang along as she made herself a ham sandwich, drowning out the loud voices moving up and down the block this afternoon. I resisted the urge to hug her.

Laid-back act aside, she's overwhelmed by her new roommie. She misses her Chinese boyfriend, Chris, who landed her this pad—no way grumpy Mr. Chin usually rents to white chicks.

With a mouth full of ham, she asked if I got nervous, being such a Delicate Girl.

I'm wiry, I said and swigged.

Aren't you scared of AIDS, even with condoms?

It's safer than one-night stands. And if you're going to be twenty and fucked up, you might as well go the whole nine yards! I winked and headed to my bedroom to dress and escape the third degree. I didn't bother to explain how cold linoleum soothes my skin when I'm freaking.

Susan's cool. When I moved in a few months ago, I worried she'd be too anal, what with her classic furniture from Pottery Barn and her trendy clothes from Barneys. But she's smoking with me, memorizing the words of "Woman to Woman," asking me to repeat lines she doesn't understand.

Chinatown is littered with little old people who want to clock me upside the head for invading their territory. They run me over on the sidewalk, their hats tied under their chins, sporting nurse shoes and canes—canes swinging everywhere. An ant colony compared to the wide sidewalks of 8th Avenue where I used to live in a cramped boarding room.

Volunteering at the Alderson Community Center keeps me sane. I wonder what the protocol is if a kid's father turns out to be a trick . . .

On the family front, Ma heard from Susan about my bobbed hair and cried. I can't believe she cried to my roommate. Whatever. I'm sick of a sweaty mane after a night of bumping and grinding. Short bangs make me look exotic. The Chinese might like me better now.

I used to assume that Ma (the Artist) liked rebellious choices, as in stripping or hair dying. She introduced me to Mae West records. And Mae demands A Guy That Takes His Time, that he be an Easy Rider. She told men to Slow Down. They jailed her for playing a prostitute on Broadway, for god's sake!

Ma even bought me a biography of Josephine Baker for my eleventh birthday. I'd flip through pictures of her topless, rolling into the Charleston, lithe and funny on stage. (I wonder if she was short. She looks petite. I like Mae West's five-foot frame because I'm only five foot two.)

The first exotic dancers I saw in New York City slinked, snarled, and hoarded their money. I saw the tough glamour of Josephine and Mae. And because I'm street smart too, I called Ma first and told her I met a stripper.

Ma ranted about how artistic expression has vanished from erotic dance and how money makes today's women weak.

I realized her naïveté. Nothing, in 1925 or 1995, stays black-and-white in the world of money and sex. Nobody stays in power long.

October 15

Yesterday I called Misty since she never calls me anymore. A year and ten months after the fact, she's still disappointed that I dropped out of college to strip.

Over the phone, she said she loves her classes, loves her friends, and loves life. Typical Misty these days. She found her calling in college—being a righteous leader of feminist poets and radical recyclers on the WVU campus. No longer the *other* haunted girl at our high school. The one with the respectably sloshed parents. The one who liked to do armpits farts and once blew a guy in a church rec room so he would take her to the prom. I know she's hiding in there, my first friend.

In high school, we used to harmonize (she was a soprano; I sang tenor), skipping through the pine forest behind my house. We ran from tree to tree and pressed our backs against the solid, scratchy trunks. Pretending to swoon at the thought of a lover—someone to watch over me . . .

As I ate Ramen noodles and listened to Misty recite her lines from *Gigi* (she'd gotten the lead, of course), those sappy images oozed into my mind. If we were together, I thought, she'd lean her back against mine and prop me up. I pictured us, looking so much alike at thirteen (both short and skinny, with brown, straight hair) that people mistook us for twins. Except that her face is softer, less dramatic. People always thought she was the prettier. I liked to chalk that up to country conservatism and the insecurity of high-school boys.

Once Misty finished singing "The Night They Invented Champagne," I blurted out my change in profession, because I'm afraid I'm imagining the whole thing. The House, the girls, and the men feel like a dream when I'm away from them. I hoped that by telling someone I trust, I'd calm down.

Hey, I said, I decided to stop stripping. I'm working at a brothel now. You know . . . hooking.

What? (Huge pause.) Are you losing your mind? I don't want to know about—

Mist, I cut in, would you listen for a sec? Hustling in the strip clubs drains me. It's like I'm cotton candy. It's like I'm pulling myself into pieces and giving myself away, melting in men's mouths.

So much conversation in the clubs.

TALK TALK TALK

Hi guys.

Whooo-wheeee! You have one fine pair of legs!

Thanks. What are you gentlemen doing this evening?

Me and my friend are here to party and talk to pretty ladies like you.

Oh, I got a couple flatterers on my hands.

Oh yeah, darling. Here's five bucks. Give my buddy the works.

I'm sorry. It's twenty for a lap dance.

Jesus Christ! A gorgeous woman like you can't cut us a deal?

MONEY MONEY MONEY MONEY

Only if you're from West Virginia.

I'm from West Virginia!

All right. What are ramps?

They're what monster trucks drive up to jump!

You obviously have to pay full price.

Where are you from in West Virginia?

The valleys. That'll be twenty dollars.

Hey, before we get down to business, tell me, Legs: where does a man find a lady to go home with him?

Sorry, don't know. And I gotta get on stage soon if you want a dance.

Oh, all right. Go ahead. Fifteen bucks, right?

No, twenty.

Fine. Go ahead.

Sorry again, but I need the money before I dance.

DANCE DANCE DANCE

(I wiggle up my dress and grind against a nubby hard-on poking up his suit pants. I push away the hands sliding up my thighs toward my butt. Unless I'm tired and the floor mother isn't monitoring. In the last months there, I grew so tired that men managed to work their fingers into me.)

TALK TALK TALK

So, where about do you gentlemen come from?

Whoa, little lady, getting personal!

Sorry (like a neighborhood gives your wife away), just trying to make conversation. You like movies?

No.

Tell me, Handsome, are you an ass or a breast man?

I'm actually a big tit-man, no offense. I'm lusting after that stripper over there. Do you know her name?

Jazz. I'll run and get her.

HUSTLING PRICKS! It'll suck your soul.

The stupid, endless sexual banter drives me mad, I said, trying to sum up the experience for Misty. I appreciate the simplicity of hooking, I added, when you compare it to the endless negotiations in clubs.

She didn't respond.

But I suppose you might not understand.

Misty sighed. I imagined her lounging on her tie-dyed bedspread, with Mean People Suck posters decorating her dorm room, shaking her head.

You're right, she said. I don't understand! I don't want to.

You don't—

You should go through your no-self-respect stage without dragging me down.

I groaned and shot myself in the face with a finger gun.

Tess, how can I love someone who doesn't love herself?

I pressed my forehead against the cool windowpane. I said, We were Wonder Twins once, and gently scraped my fingernails against the glass.

And now she's Oprah, I thought.

I try, Tess. Her voice was muffled by a pillow or blanket. But, she said with sincerity, I can't make sense of you anymore.

I need you to try harder, I said. I squinted to block out the tears.

You're in another world, she said, sounding like she was speaking to a ghost, the remains of someone she once knew.

All right, I said. If our friendship is at stake . . .

Ignoring my icy hands and the pulse pecking at my neck, I crouched down and slid backward until I was under the kitchen table. I chose to rest on a white square in the checkerboard floor. I jammed the phone between my jaw and shoulder. Kept listening for Susan, but no footsteps slowed near the apartment door.

Misty took wet breaths, sniffled; I brought my knees to my chest. I squeezed my thighs together, ready to tell her about the rape—

You've always been too self-indulgent, she said and sighed.

My legs spread flat and wide. I said that I had to go shave my toe knuckles.

I called Ma after that, looking for a bit of love.

She'd found my baby book in the attic. Banging the dust off on her jeans, she said the condition looked good. She promised to give it to me when I visited next. Reminded me that my first word was *brother* (subtle hint).

A photo of me eating a tomato at two years old made Ma laugh. And I imagined her wide smile, her hair back in a messy ponytail. I practically smelled her skin reeking of Dad's Old Spice. I could see the sweat creeping across her black tank top.

She sounds exactly the same as she did a month ago, before I wallowed in guilt, avoiding her calls. She thinks I'm a waitress in a Mexican restaurant. I just couldn't deal with keeping up the lies anymore. Did she notice?

I'm frustrated with massage, she moaned, which she says every year. Your father sold one of his harps for fourteen hundred dollars.

Wants to take a cruise. She laughed and grunted as she carried another box to the top of the stairs.

Good idea, I said. You need a break from all that clean air. Come visit me. You won't have to pay for a hotel. I'll take a week off from work.

Oh, no. We can't leave Sam, she said. Dad knows I'm right. He just gets itchy when the bad weather starts up. Besides, your brother is painting! He's on an upswing. Your mother's limited creativity is the problem because—

Why don't you move to an artist colony in Mexico? Throw Sam in the trunk, let Dad teach the locals Faulkner, but don't drink the tap water.

Oh Jesus, Tess, she said.

Before she could elaborate, I screamed, OH MY GOD! The Clearing House declared ME a million-dollar winner. I need to call the hotline.

Click.

Nothing like the support of friends and family.

October 16

Since I can't find any decent talk shows ("Grieving Mothers of Murdered Men" and "Teens Who Lie" dominate the airwaves), I'm smoking in the kitchen before I go play with the kids at the community center. Thought I'd record funny brothel tidbits for future reference.

I blank on the details of my first strip clubs—I mean I've lost the names of all the dancers, the regulars, the crazy club owners. A meandering childhood, even within one state, means my memory works in snippets. Like the memory of discovering the plywood floor of a sandbox. I scraped back the sifting sand with my bare feet and hands, frustrated by grains that squeezed through my fingers. Later, I got yelled at for emptying the slippery contents onto the grass. I can't pin that moment down to any town (we lived in six during the first nine years of my life). I can't remember whether we owned the box or if friends played with me. I just remember the excitement of exposing the rough wood.

I forget the name of the dancer who inspired me to stop cocktail-waitressing and hop on stage. A thin blonde, she wore a clingy, green dress, held a fan, and slithered to techno. She smoked gold cocktail cigarettes and put her lipstick on without a mirror. While in full split, she'd tightened one butt cheek so the flesh jumped like a pinched Nerf football. Then she'd slide a twenty-dollar bill under her g-string to where it folded and stuck out in front of her pussy, tightening her muscles to make the bill pump in and then thrust out. I admired her like I did the girls in the elementary schools who could flip their eyelids.

I never mastered either trick, though at the clubs I did whip out my childhood trump card of wrapping both my legs around my neck. Way back, other kids marveled at that contortion. And when I turned nine and Sam stopped protecting me, I stunned school yards in Charleston by embedding my nails into boys' wrists, searching for the vein, until the guilty party fell on his knees.

Ah, well. Life is full of fascinating details worth remembering. Here goes:

Prostitutes like to be called *hookers* at this particular brothel. I wonder if a different House prefers a different term. Sorry, but isn't that hilarious? Like *Native American* or *American Indian*. The fierce battle of identity rages on!

The best thing about my job is the introduction to mint-flavored condoms and a supply of gold-wrapped ones for enormous guys.

Steamers with wet, warm towels are placed in rooms to clean guys before or after.

We change and wash sheets after each session. Conscientious and hygienic hookers.

We stash *Playboy*'s in every room (alternatives to the Bible) and lubricant in every bedside table.

And judging by my two experiences, most guys are fairly considerate lovers. Diane, the madam, pointed out: What an ego trip to give a hooker an orgasm! (With this in mind, I've stopped considering dental dams. I'd lose clients.)

So crazy. I long for more people to laugh about the House with, but Misty's disgusted and Susan's overly intrigued.

Susan also doesn't share my other passions—children, talk shows, and drugstores, though she might like dancing.

Young woman seeking friends with simple sexuality. Anybody?

I miss Marie, my best big-city friend. Rehearsing some monologues at her apartment, she once persuaded me to peel down to my bra and undies so we could hang out the window and whistle at guys who walked by on Twenty-third Street. A hot July afternoon. Blasting mambo music and shaking our lacy boobies at a crowd. A dude pointed at me and yelled, Hey, I dare you to show me your ass. And I did; I swung around and mooned them, the sticky wind blowing on my butt. Marie tried not to laugh as she dragged on a joint. Cinders burned her bra.

That felt different from stripping. No weight of money, the men so far away.

Now she's given up the sex industry and lives in San Francisco with no telephone.

Whoops. I've wasted too much time reminiscing. Gotta find my lower heels. Stinky diapers, here I come!

October 18

A night of infamy. A girl caught crabs, so Diane ordered us to check for bugs by giving head before any other hanky-panky. (Regulars jump from girl to girl, brothel to brothel.) I serviced four in a row, running my nails sensually through their thick, matted pubic hair to search out insects. Yummy.

But this old dude topped off the evening, beginning with the hike up to Room 6—my first time in the '70s-style love shack. Mirrors surround the bed, and the walls are dark green. Brown, shag carpeting finishes off the sleazy appeal.

After a bit of foreplay, I heaved onto his flabby body. He moaned. I pulled up. His eyes squeezed shut behind his thick spectacles. I lowered my hips again.

He dug his fingers through my hair and shouted, Baby, you're KILLING me.

My chest tightened.

You are killing me!

He thrust up into me, again and again, almost knocking me off while his hands clenched either side of my head, still growling, You're killing me, killing me, killing.

Fingers squeezed my larynx, cracking bones—this image ran up the back of my mind.

You're fucking killing me, he shouted, his fingernails digging into my scalp. His eyes popped open.

I forced myself to silently sing "Jingle Bells" as a distraction. My tongue dried up. So I didn't have to see his frozen face, I stared at my pale ass, bobbing in the dark mirrors around us. A floating ball of flesh. Jingle bells, Batman smells.

He grabbed my hair in his fist, and I reached down and kissed him slow and deep, which made him stop. Garlic. The first one I've kissed. The softness calmed him. Soothed me.

Flashing back to the rape is productive, I decided. I'll regain a sense of control, knowing that I can ignore and overcome the fear. I'm certain.

I cried in the cab on the way home. As usual, the cabbie said nothing. On the way to work, drivers ask me how long I've lived in New York and where I'm from. I talk about West Virginia and crayfish and fend off incest jokes. The four-thirty-a.m. drivers are silent. I wait for them on a deserted corner, brick townhouses surrounding me until I slide onto the vinyl seats and ask for Chinatown, like a character from an old movie.

We glide through emptiness, roaring through yellow lights. I watch the meter, paranoid he'll rip me off like the tourist I still am. In the East Village, we pause long enough for me to see young, homeless punks who have tattoos on their chins, and I wonder about their parents and how they'll ever find work outside of Manhattan with those dark slashes on their faces.

We fly into my neighborhood. The tight turns make me grip my door handle and glance at my backpack to make sure no money or thigh highs or condoms are sliding out. I encourage him to continue down the street to my metal, gated door.

Of course, Susan woke up when I got home early this morning. She scrunched up on the leather couch and prodded me to describe the whole night. The goose bumps on her long arms and legs looked like warts, and I sensed fear pushing out the lumps of my mind, an episode coming. Excellent Malaysian Food flashed neon into the dark living room.

I shrugged and mentioned a guy digging his fingers into my scalp.

More prodding: Weren't you terrified? she asked. Without make-up, her thick lips sank into her pale face. I imagined what she wrote about me in her diary, her Emotional Release from the stress of data entry. Two roomies with our dueling diaries.

Come on, she said. Didn't he bother you at all?

I sank into an armchair, lowering my chin to my chest, trying to keep the irritation and panic at bay. Well, he reminded me of Rob a little, ripping at my hair.

She raised a pale, red eyebrow.

Susan, I said, I kept calm and quiet, and the old fart walked away happy, not a violent thought running through his sagging face.

That's all?

Yep.

Rolling her eyes, she went back to bed.

The night I moved in, we bonded with weed and red wine. I talked about Rob and the rape, quipped about my high expectation of men— no knife makes a man a Smooth Operator in my book. I also told her that I quit stripping to hook.

One deep talk, however, does not qualify her to act as my analyst. All I can say about her is that she's comfortable lounging nude in front of me, shaves off her red pubic hair, aspires to be an actress

17

(though she doesn't take classes or do auditions or send out head-shots), and doesn't like her yuppie parents much.

She's jealous because in photographs my folks look fit and hand-some with their messy hair and garden tans, wearing worn jeans and black shirts. Unlike New York artists, they sought solitude, abundant nature, and a low cost of living in order to thrive—they're country cool. Of course, Sam tries to be the odd man out, too country with his flannel shirts and bushy beard. A wannabe mountain man. And if she saw Dad these days, with his grandma-style reading glasses hang-ing from twine around his neck, she'd realize he's a big geek.

At least I'm enjoying my volunteer work. I've created a strong con-nection with a two-year-old named Beth. She's never displayed such attachment before, said my boss, Mrs. Young.

Beth's shy. I draw her out. She chases me around like a puppy, but instead of chewing on my pants, she smacks the back of my legs with her mittened hands. Brown curls tumbling over her blue eyes.

I'm actually considering buying horrid SNEAKERS to increase my mobility with the babies, make me queen of the jungle gym. As a former tomboy, with a brother as my main playmate, I'm naturally bi-ased. I rebel against the stupid color lessons and the cotton-ball art.

My childhood art lessons consisted of Ma propping me up in a cor-ner of her workspace with glitter, glue, and paper as my only entertain-ment until Sam ran home from school. Sometimes she'd hand me a bucket of papier-mâché mush and strips of cotton and show me how to wrap my baby dolls. Sounds fun, but hours of messy glitter, eating glue, and playing with mummified babies gets boring and lonely.

And later, not even the games of kiss-tag, the yearbook signatures calling me a Cool Girl, or the bathroom discussion-groups about boys could make the loneliness stop.

October 20

Four in the morning. Susan's sleeping. I turned on the fan and the radio before I collapsed onto my knotted mattress. (Broke or not, I'm buying a real bed!) The noises help me relax. So does the screwdriver under my pillow. After two fucking years, I still need a weapon to subdue my fear of (dunt, dun, dun . . .) RAPISTS!

If I had the nerve, I'd punch myself in the face—bam!—knock the thick, brown mucous loose and shake myself by the neck until the foulness drained out of my head, down my throat, and I'd sit on the toilet and shit for hours. Yahoo! Fuck you, fear!

On a happier note, a particularly nice guy came to the House tonight.

The girls filed into the Living Room, excited because City Gary was young and handsome, a true rarity. Shy guy, blushing.

He picked me. Preening, I led him up the stairs, explaining that my name is Estelle, a name I chose because I associate it with old ladies and French chicks, and I like the idea of being an old French prostitute. I brought him to the southwestern room.

As I dimmed the lights, I teasingly ordered, Get Completely Comfortable; I like my men young and sockless.

Then I ran to the basement to get the scoop. Well, Diane said, this is his first visit, so be careful. Might be a cop, another girl said. Don't acknowledge the money. Someone shouted that I could not discuss sex.

I slinked back upstairs, expecting a gun or handcuffs. Instead, I was greeted by this long, toned body with this smooth, big dick, and I was impressed. He sat cross-legged, naked in the middle of the bed. Eager. Most guys lie under the covers.

I asked him how long he wanted to stay, and he said, An hour, and nodded to a pile of bills on the nightstand.

Seconds later, I stripped in front of City Gary.

We made out, easily, like we'd practiced. The only thing was . . . no discussion of sex. He asked about my fantasies (guys love dirty, stupid stories), what pleased me the most, what positions I liked, but I'd only giggle. If I broke my silence, the cops would kick down the door and drag everyone, as naked as plucked chickens, down to the station.

He drove me to orgasm after orgasm. He chanted, Talk to me, talk to me. Stayed for two hours. Incredible! Hands down, the best sex I've ever had.

And after, I wobbled down to the basement to tell everyone my story. As it turned out, the instruction not to talk about sex only applied before he handed me the cash!

I hope he stops by again. He said that I look like Winona Ryder, which I liked, though my eyes are light brown and my jawline is sharper.

He asked me what I needed to consider him my Best Client Ever.

Spoil me, I said.

So he gave me a hundred-dollar tip. A rich romantic. Sigh.

October 22

Ma's phone call caught me half asleep and off guard this morning, or else I would've let the machine pick up.

Sam's drinking again, she said as a greeting. I'm afraid to let him come for Thanksgiving.

I heard her smacking a spoon in her hand, probably striding around the kitchen.

I don't know why she acts surprised. I restrained myself from shouting, Woman, your son is an alcoholic! He's always drinking!

She stilled. Tess. You can't be too busy to come home and talk to your brother. You said the restaurant owes you a week off. Thanksgiving? Christmas?

I opened the fridge and cracked a can of pop. I asked, Is this the upswing you described?

That managed to piss her off.

He is painting, she said. He just needs a boost.

I explained that with rent, bills, buying a futon, and paying off my credit card, affording the holiday flight would be impossible. I'll visit on my birthday. I'll be legal then, I said. Sam and I can go drinking together so neither one of us feels like a loser on Valentine's Day.

You're not funny, Tess, she said.

I plopped onto one of our kitchen chairs. Ma always cries for help, only to drop the subject as soon as she discovers a new massage technique or the hottest women's issue. Or she waits for me to cave and call Sam.

Can't I just come for my birthday? I asked.

Honey, please. He yells anytime I offer to clean his place. (Her big way of helping him.) He won't open the door. Her voice, like a train, picked up force: Last night, he drove here completely drunk and parked in the middle of the lawn. Your father was forced to carry him inside. (I could picture Sam's work boots dragging across the grass, his greasy, black hair flopping against Dad's arm.) I was forced to move the station wagon in my nightgown so the neighbors wouldn't see it in the morning.

Ma. Dark hair swirling around her long neck. Her broad shoulders sticking out in the cool air, creating shadows over her white, cotton nightgown. She'd direct a slumping Dad to lift Sam. Dad would want to wake his son so Sam would take responsibility for his behavior. Just get him inside, she'd say.

His girlfriend is trash, Ma muttered.

She reported that with Trash's help (shopping for his toilet paper and such) Sam mostly stays in his apartment. He loads up on free food while washing dishes at Mike's. Oh sure, he walks across the street to buy beer, as if he needs more calories!

Ma sees gaining weight as Sam's ultimate crime.

You bring him out to the country, she stated firmly, and make him take a walk with you. Please. You two could climb the boulders in Ray's field. Please.

Too sleepy to fight, I stopped her by saying I'd look into fares. She quieted, hedging her bets.

He must be in bad shape for her to say Please. I peered out my window to watch the cars cramming through Chinatown. The angry bellow of horns.

I thought about our neighbors outside of Elkins—families who live five miles up the road—the ones who lift a finger in greeting, as if to say, Hey, I hardly know ya since you moved here at the age of thirteen. I like your brother though. He's broody, but a nice guy. Catch ya next Halloween.

I told Ma I might come sooner rather than later. Miss the holiday fares.

Thank you, dear.

I can't avoid her crazy love forever. And I miss Sam.

Later, I ate a depressing lunch with Peter. He's home for a long weekend. Enjoying Dartmouth, but feels out of place after NYU—not as many gay actors.

I told him about my shaking attacks and how the test for hyper-thyroid came back negative, which allows for the possibility that I'm going insane. Well, the nurse didn't say that, but she offered no other explanation.

While telling Peter about an episode, I freaked in the restaurant. My heart sped up. I'm dying, I thought. I swallowed over and over, pulling spit down so I wouldn't choke. The candle on the black table seemed fake, as if it might crumble into powder if I tried to wrap my fingers around it.

I burst outside, into a light drizzle.

Hey, don't worry, you're fine, Peter said when he caught up. Then he yelled, Look at me! I'm singing in the rain, just singing in the rain . . . He sang and danced to distract me, looking like a young George from *Seinfeld* bounding up and down the sidewalk.

Excuse me. The landlord just called us back about our rotted shower.

And I should mention that a few pricks chose me last night. One stood out, with a new level of asshole-dom, but I'm not dwelling.

I'm in a pissy mood after a shitty day, so I'll stop writing and drink a glass of wine.

I wonder if Jenny Jones is hosting a makeover marathon. Ciao.

October 23

It is 4:47 a.m. according to my friendly alarm clock. I'm tired, cold, and in a grouchy mood left over from my last entry. So I've decided not to censor the bad crap.

The new level of asshole-dom I mentioned? That was a small, pro-fessorial-looking gentleman. I led him to sleazy Room 6. And with only a half hour paid for, I jumpstarted business, stroking him. But we ran into trouble. Not another, I thought—the land of slug dicks. Blowjob time rolled around, and giving head when they're soft is the worst because the condom makes squishy noises and your lips feel like they're massaging a fat, dead worm. On top of all that, the loose rubber is like sucking on a piece of Saran Wrap.

My jaw started to ache, and with no erection in sight after ten minutes, he admitted that he did coke at this party, which would've been nice to know before. He proceeded to describe a certain trick that always got him off.

So, to make a long story short, I smacked him a few times and rubbed my feet in his face until he came.

Lord . . . I disturb me. What went wrong in my life that I find myself smashing my toes into guy's eyes as they shudder with orgasm? Or is it perfectly healthy for me to help guys fulfill their fantasies? I want to think I'm helping them.

I'm not mentally disabled, but I don't know what to say or think.

Ma gave me the birds-and-bees talk when I was young. She told me the basic facts when I was eight and thought babies emerged from the belly button. She stressed the importance of the orgasm when I turned twelve and my breasts were nothing more than nubs.

I should've pressed her further. I should've sat on our swing set and chewed gum, saying, Yeah, yeah, I got the clitoris thing, but what happens if Ken wants Barbie to spank him or rub her feet in his face—what do I do? And what about the boys who like to hurt you—how do I head them off at the pass? Do I head them off?

Demanding an orgasm is like learning the doggy-fucking-paddle. What if I'm called upon to do water ballet?

I cannot go back to stripping. The last time I worked at the Pussy Cat, I undulated as usual, but my brain shut down. I literally got nauseated at the idea of hustling. I sat on a bench in the dressing room as music banged through the floorboards. Made fifty bucks for seven hours of work.

Damn it, I'm shaking. Keep away, nightmares. I bite back!

There once was a monster named Ned.
He hid under a little girl's bed.
He lay there all night,
Waiting for a big bite,
Only to be KICKED in the head.

October 24

I'm a wreck. I vow not to smack another customer.

And I want a companion. When I'm lonely, the wind seems to blow right through me.

Sam and I used to play King of the Mountain in Ray's boulder field. We'd climb to the top of these ten-foot-high rocks, finding fingerholds in the angled walls. They're fossilized dinosaur turds, Sam claimed. Honest, he'd say, honest. Don't you notice the faint odor?

I thought he was so funny.

On top of the boulder, we'd assume sumo-wrestling positions, trying to push each other off, carefully of course, so the other person could twist and land on their feet. We never got hurt, just worked up an appetite. Lunch was part of the ritual, which meant a PB & J, a Twix candy bar, and three Cokes for me; three beers and Kentucky

Fried Chicken for Sam. We'd discuss our wrestling techniques and how so much depended on solid footing, analyze Harrison Ford's appeal in *Star Wars* versus *Indiana Jones*.

During moments of silence, the sound of the nearby stream, sliding over rocks and tumbling against the dirt banks, reached our ears. Ray's cows filed past, below us, their tails twitching. The hovering flies lunged at our food, sending us into a new battle, reviving us.

Two months ago, I tried working at the dry cleaners. Most country people are smart enough to buy clothes that can go in a regular washer, but in New York, I cater to the rich. Hello there, starch?, tag clothes, ring up the register, sit down, and wait, wait, wait—again, again, and again.

The day I quit, I headed back to my apartment so restless that I tore my stack of newspapers and magazines into shreds. The plan to create homemade confetti ended with my bedroom floor and mattress coated in bits of paper. A ticker-tape parade. Scissors shredding. Books, too. Hands black with ink.

Then I sprinted up Canal Street. A white chick running hard in a red flamenco skirt. The soles of her feet pink and hot, she paused to catch her breath. She. Her. Me.

At least the House drowns out my crazier urges. I've traded emotional explosions for the urge to whisper, I'm a prostitute, to upper-crust women on the subway. I itch to tell people that we walk among them, like vampires. I will one day. My wild side is genetic.

In the blissful era before Sam's DUI, Ma tied sponges to her feet and sang opera along with West Virginia Public Radio while she stomped out paint. Dad laid canvases on the attic floor for her to pound, sponge, or splash. One smaller canvas was framed and stood on her easel, the last one to be painted, where Ma's reality would find its space. Blurred subjects arose as her final vision. Couples and children stretched out like highway headlights photographed with a slow, blinking lens.

As a teenager, I expressed my creativity by masturbating on the wooden bedroom floor because my bed squeaked. No one would have heard, but the possibility terrified me into elaborate disguises, like pillows over my face and under my butt as I snuck fingers below my waistband.

Afterward, I'd blast "Me and Bobby McGee," line my lips and eyes in black, and throw on my red bathrobe with peacocks embroidered along the hemline. Winking at the mirror, I'd dance, or sometimes follow the scent of merlot and wailing of arias to the attic where Dad had cut skylights in the walls and filled them with glass and treetops for his wife, the rough woman he followed.

I'd sit cross-legged across from Ma, sharing the wine, laughing about primitive painting urges. She'd sit on a fringed pillow, legs spread, her feet propped on pieces of newspaper. Grayish liquid slid down the sides of her ankles. Pieces of twine held the damp sponges in place, squeezing her feet so tight that thick, purple veins strained between the ropes. She'd finger paint her gray temples brown when no one was watching, claiming she was simply messy.

Sometimes I'd visit her when I felt tired, wearing plain jeans and a T-shirt. We'd turn the music down low and whisper for the sake of my teenage heart.

But always, after twenty minutes, her eyes would slip to the tray of colors on the floor, and the sponges would start bouncing up and down. Her sentences would begin to end with upward, encouraging tones, and I'd know paint and opera tugged at her. I'd leave with a dry mouth, a few words still stuffed inside.

Missing her. I even miss the half-empty feeling.

October 26

Susan is so socially aggressive that even I'm shocked by what roars out of her frosted lips. Maybe it's just the thrill of being newly single, but last night she actually nudged a guy in the side and said, Man, what I wouldn't give for a bottle of champagne!

Before we left the apartment, she did fifty sit-ups and yanked her beautiful red hair into a ponytail that stretched out nonexistent wrinkles (she's only twenty-six). I like the girl, but streaks of blush create a joker smile that doesn't ease until Noxzema facial wash prepares her for bed.

Admittedly, she's not the only freak. At the clubs, I protect myself from the meat market by rocking and bumping in the center of the dance floor. Yet, as soon as my swaying hips slow, my eyes scan the lounge for rich, needy, old men.

Last night, I managed to flirt with a young, Spanish guy wearing a T-shirt so tight I could've bitten his black nipple without a second look. Unfortunately, he barely spoke English.

Damn it, why can't a young, American man glance my way and realize I'm his soul mate? A sweet guy who will whisk me off to a farm to procreate—four to six offspring, minimum. Dark-haired beauties with green eyes, running through hayfields, chasing fireflies. I already save clothes because I figure my girls will want to play dress-up. Each time they tug my skirt, I'll reveal a strand of fake pearls, another pink wig.

City Gary, who still pursues the title of My Best Client, galloped back into my arms tonight. He's going through a divorce and admitted that the marriage failed because he tied the knot out of fear, not love. I suspect he's asserting his new freedom with me.

Gary massaged my back and tickled me with stories about his obsessive search for Robert Johnson relics. During his hunt, he's flown to obscure towns in Mississippi and seen men with no teeth; rabid dogs; boxes buried behind outhouses; and beautiful, old records that had been half burnt to wash away the stink of the devil, with whom Johnson reportedly struck a deal.

Finally, I rolled over and asked him, What kind of deal are you striking?

You see, I grew up on Robert Johnson. Dad loves him. And Gary's green eyes match the blue pines behind my parents' home. We'd make beautiful babies together.

Gently tugging one of my earlobes, Gary asked me (many guys do) why I work in the brothel. And I answered honestly for once, figuring that he'd talked straight with me.

I said, I want to explore my sexuality, I need money, and I feel constrained by normal jobs. In the dry cleaners, I dreaded the chit-chat—How are the kids, Mr. Robins? Good weather today. Did the medium amount of starch work well?

Ugh. Life's everyday inquiries wear on me. They feel like lies too heavy to bear. I'm only comfortable with people's raw emotions. Listen, I said, I crossed over to the gritty side on a night two years ago, and now I'm not tolerant of anything else. Surprised at my own candor, I tried to slide off the bed, caught unaware by the comfort of him.

Gary held me and kissed my eyelids, my nose, my neck. He said that he escapes his upper-class world by crashing seedy bars and getting loaded with strangers. His best friend is an ex-con who was charged with armed robbery. After the bars close, the two tear around the city in Gary's BMW, running red lights and talking their way out of speeding tickets.

He's the reason I'm achy—romantic longings. His number is on a piece of paper in my purse, but I can't call. I know better.

October 27

Earlier today, I called home to discuss when I might fly in, and Sam picked up. Four months since we last spoke.

Hey, Sis, he said. What's up?

I'm good, good, I said, taken aback by his sudden proximity, his cigarette-smoked voice. I stumbled through, Long time, no hear. What are you doing home? Where are the parents?

Not here, he said. He sniffed (and I imagined he shrugged his shoulders, the gesture he's used to look tough since he was eight and made his first enemy in Sean Dotes).

I tried to think of something to say as my tea kettle started to whistle. Finally I asked him how he thought Ma and Dad were doing these days.

Nothing that liquor or a straight jacket won't cure, he said and chuckled. They're up in arms over me, as usual.

Surprise, surprise, I said. I heard the television flip on, and I huffed, Guess you're not interested in speaking to your long-lost sister.

Ya know I gotta keep totally occupied. But I'm listening.

His long arms and legs thumped against the folds of the couch.

Tell me again, he said, about the wonders of Chinese sandals.

Digging through my cabinets to find a teabag, I smiled and said, Screw you, dork.

Hey. I know we got a reputation here in West Virginia, but I don't like to encourage the stereotype, thank you kindly.

You're gross, I said. And, shaking my head at his twang, I accidentally tipped my kettle; half of the water landed in my mug, while the rest flooded the counter. I jumped and shrieked. Water gushed and then trickled onto our floor. I pressed a dish towel into the steaming puddle.

Hell, you're busy, Sam said.

I just spilled some water, I said, kneeling to finish wiping the floor. Any news? I asked. You still got the pirate beard? (He doesn't like his Brando mug. Says it gives people the wrong impression.)

Yeah, but I promise to shave if you come home and chill out Ma.

Alright already, I said. I will. Who is this girlfriend I've heard about?

You heard about Trashy Terri already? You and Ma are busybodies. She works at the Kodak factory. You wouldn't know her—too old.

What's the attraction?

The usual.

Which is?

She puts out, of course.

I called him a pervert. He laughed and lectured me on avoiding boys that are nasty like his chick. Watch out for roach-infested city boys, he joked, and I leaned back on my heels and hooted because of the crab scare. And he didn't even want to know why I was amused.

Then I didn't know what to say, so I went quiet. I kicked the wet rag aside. When I blew into my tea, an oval dip formed. The dark water sent my breath up and out. I blew straight down, and the dip deepened.

He asked, What's wrong? I only hear stories of Miss Well-Adjusted. Tess is doing fine, Ma says. Loves waitressing. Adores New Yor—

I'm still stripping. Don't tell Ma and Dad.

You ever known me to tattle?

No. I guess that isn't one of your many flaws.

Ha, ha, Sam said and then added, One last thing before I go: keep your head up, all right? You're great, so don't let Ma or those shit-heads at the clubs tell you otherwise.

I told him that he's great, too . . . just kind of a fuck-up. I always try to make him laugh before he disappears.

My big baby brother. I don't know if I can be happy if he isn't.

He used to spend hours pushing me around Berkeley Springs in a baby carriage, relieving his newborn sister's colic. At only six years old, he would guide me down the main street to the spring taps where the waters ran clear and cool. I'd smile and smack the dribble and suck the wetness off my fat fingers. Sometimes Sam would even ditch first grade to help Ma care for me. He'd sneak me into the old movie theater that we lived behind, entrancing me with Clint Eastwood's squint and the sound of horses pounding across a plain.

I managed to scare Ma and Dad away, but not Sam.

Years later, in another town, he taught me how to ride a bike. He sprinted hard, his huge sneakers slipping on gravel, scraping his knee to give me that last push. And I pedaled on my own for two seconds before he needed to push me again, and again, and again. At the end of the day, we were scraped and not too proud.

Sam figured out how to make hot chocolate. I sat on a stool watching the white milk swirl in the silver pan, testing the temperature with my finger when he instructed. Ma painted upstairs, Dad was out carving. I remember the warm washcloth he held against my palms, raw from smacking the pavement as I fell.

Whenever we moved, tired and hungry as he was, his hair matted from sleeping in the car, Sam searched for my stuffed animals before he unpacked his own toys. The last couple of times, he didn't unpack most of his stuff, figuring we wouldn't stay long enough for him to bother, but he still helped me. Then we played dolls as Ma and Dad hauled the furniture.

He gave me advice on how to let go. Don't write letters, he'd say gruffly. Leave no trace.

Unconsciously, his advice followed my parents' pattern. They never kept in touch, and when we did run into an old neighbor (inevitable in our little state), the conversation was awkward, as if my parents had stood the person up for reasons never made clear. If my parents had been a man, they would've been a player with commitment issues. They talked about not wanting to be tied down.

I turned nine. Sam was fifteen. We moved to Charleston, leaving Lewisburg behind, like all the other places, and he stopped helping me, paying attention. Four years later, drunk and depressed because he'd flunked out of college, Sam barely talked in the car as we moved from Charleston to Elkins.

I miss him.

Pandy is purring next to me, sweet as ever. I did book a flight home. Maybe I can help Sam. Or not. Either way, come four days, I'll be relaxing in the country.

33

October 28

I grooved on a great mood until Misty called to make sure we're cool. She said she's sorry she called me names and that she worries about my Safety. She didn't mean to piss me off, but she thinks I deserve a guy who loves me.

Naturally, I agree. Nice men, however, drop into Misty's lap every day. She doesn't appreciate her luck.

I described the quality of the House: On the Upper East Side. So safe. Diane and Cara, the phone girl, stay in the basement regulating the traffic. The men, who are only referred by other customers, call from the corner payphone and then walk over. Video cameras at the door monitor the guys as they approach and recite their code names into an intercom.

Sometimes clients forget their codes and are turned away. No bending the rules in this whorehouse! Each room is equipped with a powerful shower you can use before or after The Dirty Deed. And one room sports a bidet, which I love. A tower of safe sex spiraling to the sky.

Misty groaned, but she laughed too. She blew me a kiss and told me to be careful before she hung up. Felt good to convince her that hooking isn't totally evil.

Close to eight hundred dollars a week puts a dent in my debt. (Since I quit dancing, three months of city rent, phone bills, gas bills, student loans, and food money have maxed out my credit cards.)

I look forward to the rest, though, a break in the humping marathon, to walk in a country house where the wood moves and breathes with you. Manhattan is hard and confining once you're here. Cement doesn't give, so each step jars the body. The traffic forms a Berlin Wall, and I suspect that once a person leaves, they won't come back.

I'm also daydreaming about City Gary a lot. He's screwed up, but we match. He wants to treat me to the most expensive dinner in town.

I want clothes. How cool for a man to know your taste and size, and select the perfect dress for you to wear? I know I sound disgustingly *Pretty Woman*.

Unfortunately, I'm not dumb enough to fall for my own fantasies. (He'd probably choose a snakeskin bodysuit.) But since I can't date Gary, I certainly look forward to our sessions together. He's sweet, and with a mint condom on his dick, he's the anthropomorph of Junior Mints! Ha! I'm crass.

My new futon arrived today, and I'm so pleased. It takes up 90 percent of my bedroom. I'm rolling on the mattress right now, eating Skittles.

October 29

Slow night. I lounged and watched the strangely drab Diane flirt with customers on the phone, tantalizing them with stories of girls they might enjoy. I'm fascinated.

The interview (way back when) blew my mind.

To sit naked in a plush bedroom, anticipating the mystery man/ woman who will judge you as a possible hooker . . . then this huge lady lowers herself into view, her ankles hanging over the edge of her shoes. She wears jogging suits, no makeup, and her thin, brown hair lies limp on her head. Yet, she used to hook and knows her shit.

After I twirled around naked, she handed me a robe and proceeded to talk for an hour, explaining how we pose as a catering business for taxes and other official stuff. Only one girl in her eight years as madam has been raped (better statistics than the real world). Say No to uncomfortable requests, she said, and leave the room if you sense a threat.

Diane also warned, in a matter-of-fact tone, that I'd never be my parents' little girl again.

We sat in the dim light of Room 1, me sweating nervously, her describing the prison pack, containing snacks and deodorant that we stash by the telephone in case the cops ever bust us. We plead innocent. They bail us out and pay any fines.

I listened so attentively, she was surprised when I accepted her offer. You seemed too careful, she admitted later, handing me my first pack of gold condoms.

Christ, I realize this is a hard and destructive job. I'm not stupid. I'm hanging onto a sheet, and the cotton is tearing above me while I sink into darkness. I know.

But I crave the dark and perverse. To fuck fifty guys, one after another, to pound my head against the floor until I give myself a lobotomy, to fall all the way into the pit and feel the slimy bottom just once.

The fire must burn me to make the attraction die.

I want to move on! I want to crush the emptiness.

Oh, god, I'm crying. So tired. Numb, except when fear throbs to life or this hole inside my chest pulses. I'll self-destruct or get over the hump.

I'm lonely. The girls who make friends and integrate the business into their lives seem happier, more normal.

I like Sarah and Erin, who both started recently. A voluptuous girl from Louisiana, Erin cracks jokes and insists on reading *Playboy* profiles for amusement. Sarah is shy and real sweet. Maybe friendships will bloom.

October 31: Halloween

Last day before vacation, and we dressed up like Bond girls. I bought a toy gun that sparks and makes a whirring sound when you pull the trigger. Erin froze to death in a leopard-print bathing suit. We all wanted to be called Pussy Galore.

The guys, of course, loved it—walking through a spiderweb strung across the door to find us sprawled out on beanbags, illuminated by the red bulb we screwed into the overhead.

Janice, the girl who's worked here the longest—forty years old and famous for her blowjobs—put whoopee cushions under the couch cushions. One guy defended himself, clenching his complimentary bag of Halloween candy until we explained the joke.

Diane also let us tie howling goblins to the handrail leading upstairs. The goblins didn't pick up the vibrations of our footsteps, so we kept slapping their horned heads as we passed. She banned decorations from the bedrooms, unfortunately.

I wore a tube top and a miniskirt that zips up the side. I outlined my eyes in charcoal liner and wore fake vampire teeth, the best feature.

Please, I snarled to the guys, let me keep the fangs. They paused for a second and then dismissed me with a guffaw and a slap on my shoulder.

Usually, we're supposed to wear Normal Stuff—in the guise of normal catering girls. But I don't own Normal Stuff. Once the temperature drops, my headpiece is a fur hat with earflaps.

Tonight, Diane scowled as I pushed it on and skipped out the door. Janice shared my cab. Across the backseat, she said, Diane slaps girls, even pushed one down the steps a year ago.

I joked, I can't imagine what they did to move her; she appears to be beached on her recliner.

Janice didn't respond, and before I figured out a way to delete my bitchy remark, we arrived at my building.

I'm exhausted, my thoughts scattered. Young, fucked up, and doing it in style. People must think, She's fucked up, but—wow—look at that hat!

Thank god for my vacation.

We'll see if I can look my folks in the eye.

A bulletin from the community center: Remember how my connection with little Beth impressed the teachers? Her parents had her hearing checked, and the doctors discovered serious inner-ear blockage. She barely heard a thing. But because I make such deliberate eye contact with kids, she managed to read my lips and facial expressions.

Using hearing aids this afternoon, her interactions with other kids skyrocketed. I acted busy when she wanted to play. Good for her to branch out.

Big day tomorrow. And I hate flying! I'll drink a lot on the plane.

November 1995

November 1

In my room resting after Dad picked me up from the airport in Morgantown. We drove in silence through the chilled countryside, barren except for the occasional white house tucked in the woods or a tractor in the fields. (Country roads, take me home.) Dad said that I should ignore Ma's meddling. That Sam's hospitalization still has her in rare form. He twisted a bushy eyebrow between his fingers and complained, in his monotone, that Ma tries to control Sam even though counselors advise them to let him hit rock bottom. Allow him to make his own bed, and there he'll lie until he decides to get up.

No doubt, I said. And we left it at that.

Now I'm lying on my childhood bed, a twin, missing my king-size futon. A draft creeps into the room and blows on my neck. Hair rises off my arms.

Sam's not here, but in a couple of days, Ma is throwing an early Thanksgiving dinner to lure him—after my aunt Kate and her kids leave.

I'd hoped to avoid the holiday meal. We celebrated our last carefree one years ago in Lewisburg, before Sam got so angry about moving to Charleston that he smashed out his bedroom windows with a baseball bat. My dislike of the Puritans aside, the food nauseates me.

Also, Thanksgiving two years ago was when Sam and I drove to Mark Fiser's party, a classic rape-movie opening. We stepped out of the dry, hot station wagon. Guns N' Roses blared from a random stereo, and everyone drank behind the open doors of trucks and cars parked in the field, huddling together to block the cold.

The crowd retreated to an enormous barn with bales of hay stacked ten to twenty feet high. The wind picked up a corner of the tin roof, shaking it like a rug, creating a sound similar to a track team sprinting up metal gymnasium stairs. High-school acquaintances talked about their first semester at college. Rhonda was already engaged to another eighteen-year-old at Bob Jones University. My old smoking buddy Daniel was thinking about dropping out and focusing on his pottery. I was enjoying NYU but still wondered if formal training was necessary for acting. On a basic level, acting is about learning to be in the moment, reacting naturally as a character with specific needs and maybe a few tics. I wasn't certain that practicing to place my tongue on the roof of my mouth in order to pronounce my s's would help me as much as simply going to auditions.

An hour after we arrived, the wind died down, and people built a campfire. I remember red embers cracking, floating like fireflies in the air above our heads. Sam laughing, mesmerizing my high-school classmates with his bad-boy, handsome presence, straddling a bale of hay, a beer tucked in his shirt pocket. He smacked his hands on his thighs, playing percussion for the five guitars picking at a Paul Simon song. Soon, packing for school pressed on my mind, but Sam waved me away twice, pointing to a jar of moonshine working its way around the fire.

That stuff'll make you go blind, I said to him.

Not much in this world worth looking at, he said.

I stood on the edge of the group and saw Misty and her friend Rob in the distance.

Once Rob got me alone, I threw up my Thanksgiving dinner.

I dropped out of NYU over Christmas break.

November 2

I played with Aunt Kate's kids today. It's like living at the community center. They clambered all over, kissing me with their Popsicle-covered lips. I blew bubbles for them to smack in midair. We sang "Puff the Magic Dragon" while jumping on the couch, jumping on my bed, and, finally, jumping on Ma and Dad's queen-size bed. In the evening, a cartoon entranced them. Watching the characters chitter-chatter, I slumped asleep on a peanut-butter sandwich lying on the arm of the couch. Relaxed. Warm.

I step outside to smoke occasionally. But because this autumn has been cold for West Virginia, I prefer to lean out my bedroom window so my legs stay toasty.

The new furnace works beautifully. Until a year ago, we relied mostly on the huge fireplace, which centers the living-room area and is boxed in by the TV and couch. Another third of the main room is the open kitchen, marked off and surrounded by wood counters. The walnut table that Dad made with Sam indicates the dining area. Sam's initials are scratched on the underside. The story goes that I demanded to hammer in a few nails, too, bruising my tiny thumb. The finger swelled and turned a deep purple. Mom and Dad say it looked just like a large grape. One of those childhood tales that supposedly defines you, one that is pulled out of the archives as an example of either my fearlessness or my stupidity.

On opposite sides of the main room shoot two halls, holding the bedrooms. Sam used to sleep across from me during his periodic moves home. (He was nineteen and trying to gain some independence when we moved here.) Of course, the attic is Ma's workspace, and we store everything in the basement. Everything, that is, that made it with us this far.

I call this place Home.

The long porch is my favorite spot. At fifteen, I bought a hammock with my savings and lay cradled there for the next two summers, scooting over to let Misty on. We hung out and read books. We marched in pro-choice rallies and bonded over liberal ideals. Oddballs compared to most of our peers. I secretly liked that her parents were cocktail-hour alcoholics, though she'd never admit it. She only rolled her eyes when we walked downstairs at night to grab a snack from her fridge, only to find her parents passed out at the table, two well-worn martini glasses in front of them, olives drying up at the bottom of each.

We had an unspoken pact to never become like those around us. I worry more about reaching that goal now.

November 3

My cousins headed back to Indiana. A fun visit. A salad spoon was enough to transform me into a bandleader, and I swept them into elaborate productions. Their legs swung, accompanied by squeals. And after finishing a number, they bowed and giggled through fingers.

I'd shout, Again!

Their mom occasionally requested that we Shut Up!

I said, Kids are supposed to be noisy, Aunt Kate.

At least do the fox-trot that I taught them, she said dismissively.

Ma thinks that Aunt Kate is tacky but feels obliged to entertain her since Dad can't manage to have a civilized conversation with his sister. Her conservative politics irritate him. His entire family irritates him—Italian Catholics from Chicago. Lots of alcoholics, his father included. They're all in construction or car sales, except for him—their little genius who won a scholarship at the University of Chicago, married another rebel Catholic, and rejected them all.

But over the years, Dad's star gradually faded. With no tenure and no books, his ability to distance them with snorts of impatience and literary references lessened. They grew amused by their brother's haughtiness (I'm embarrassed to witness it, knowing he's not usually such a dick). The six siblings grew accustomed to it, as they had grown accustomed to their father's disappointment with them except my father.

Having applied himself early and gotten promotions, Grandpa spent most of his life as the head of a construction crew that built houses for a large development firm. He took this lofty position to mean that if he hung out with the workers beneath him, he would be lowering himself and his family.

He led a fairly lonely life, according to my mother. He read as many newspapers as he could buy and yelled the information that he learned to the horde of children who wrestled in the living room or jammed up the hallways to put on their snow boots as they made their way outside.

Only when Dad was born late in the marriage did he have an audience and a hope. But eventually Dad ran from Grandpa too, away from his expectations, his alcohol, his vicarious joy and pain with every one of Dad's achievements and failures.

I wonder if that isn't why he let Mom decide all our moves, pull him from job to job—because in the end it was easier than facing the consequences of his own decisions.

I only remember meeting Grandpa a few times. I saw him last at the age of twelve. I remember that he sipped on shots of whiskey and shuffled as he walked, followed Dad around to his shop, and drove with him to the school where Dad taught kids how to prepare for the GED. I remember him slowly sitting down on the floor next to me and Sam to play cards, offering us a taste of the whiskey and Coke that he'd mixed for himself, and us refusing, sticking out our tongues. And finally, I remember him saying how lucky we were.

You two, he said, have the smartest man in the world as your father. That man didn't bother with killing himself for tenure or trying to be the next Einstein. Instead he's making beautiful instruments and helping kids in need. I never got to contribute in that way, no sir. I didn't have the vision your father has, to try life a new way. But, boy, is it a thing to watch.

Sam and I smiled and nodded the way kids do when they know older people are full of shit but don't have the heart to break it to them.

November 4

Every morning Dad quietly drives off to Davis and Elkins College to teach Melville, but he spends evenings in the shop, making harps, escaping thought.

Ma didn't schedule any massages because she wants to spend time babying me.

Our conversations strain, heave, and collapse. I'm not dating, I stopped attending acting workshops, the community center is only interesting if you know the kids, and all I can say about work is that waitressing in a Mexican restaurant is boring.

We sit in the kitchen and talk about Sam's drinking.

Well, today she did most of the talking, stirring a huge pot of black-bean soup, whacking the wooden spoon against the rim, sighing, taking deep yoga breaths and asking me if I'd confront him.

I hunched down. Ma, I can't.

She wiped her oven mitt across her forehead. Why not?

You talk to him for once, I said. He's obviously avoiding me. Anyway, he's gotta decide for himself. I just want to let him know that I support him by . . . doing something together, if he ever comes out of hiding! I stared at the refrigerator. The magnetic poetry formed the phrase: Stagnant Putrid Swaying.

Fine, Tess, fine. You're probably right, as usual.

She got pissed at me, as usual.

I asked her who wrote the line on the fridge.

She did.

I should be kinder. The fear for Sam pulls her skin tight, her lips thin.

When Dad phoned six months ago and said that Sam had had an alcohol-induced seizure, I flipped out, too. And the news brought on my first attack.

So, until I control my body again, I'm resisting Ma's worries.

She's lost fifteen or twenty pounds. Cheekbones jutting, she gnaws at her beautiful, thick nails.

Later: Tonight, Sam attended the fake Thanksgiving dinner that Ma threw. He was puffy, worn, and white around his mug (kept his promise to shave the pirate beard), and he laughed and smacked his hand on the tablecloth a lot. He made the silver jump at my restaurant story about a man who discreetly chewed on his paper napkin, eating it from each corner inward, and then asked for another.

I made up some emergency stories on the flight.

Sam drank water and told me that he likes his job as a dishwasher, doesn't care that he lost his job at the garage. Thirty pounds heavier than last year—losing Handsome fast. Sam's twenty-six now, and I wonder if he'll make it to thirty. I wonder if I will.

Yeah, probably. I'm tougher, never liked drugs much. My will wouldn't let me kill myself. Even Sam does it slowly, subtly, sneaking up on himself.

Ma hovered, wearing lipstick and a cream blouse in honor of his presence, refilling the water glasses at least six times.

I felt like saying, Ma, you can lead a man to water, but . . .

Dad smiled at me or stared at the front door.

Toward the end of the meal, as I picked at the crust on my rebellious tuna sandwich, Ma shooed away Sam's claims that he had to leave early.

You can't, she said. Your little sister flew from New York to see you.

She went on about the Boring Parents retiring for the night and letting the siblings bond.

Sam didn't look at me after that. He kept touching his newly shaved jaw. The pale skin seemed translucent, babyish, in contrast to the thick bones beneath.

Before dessert, Dad took Sam out to the shed to show him a rocking chair that he'd finished. Next thing you know, I heard Dad's truck pulling out of the driveway with my brother in the passenger seat.

Where are you going? Ma shouted out the front door to Sam's waving hand.

A whispered argument lashed through the house forty-five minutes later when Dad reappeared without Sam.

Sam's face is ruddy.

If he stopped drinking, would the red go away?

November 5

The leaves sprinkling our yard are frozen stiff.

I'm curled on the porch swing, wrapped in blankets, my nose cold.

Dad walked out a little while ago and sat down next to me. Sorry about last night, he said, taking off his reading glasses. Your mother fixes her heart on how things should go and forgets that people might differ in opinion.

I know, I said, pulling the blanket snug around my neck.

He stroked my hair (I flinched—too much touching recently) and left me alone.

My body, my body feels better. No rough fingering that you don't redirect for fear of smaller tips. When I dream, I don't dream of dicks and toxic semen sliding near a scratch on my finger.

I dream about calm, bare trees. I dream about dry ditches along dirt roads where frogs look for water.

I work as a hooker in a far-away place, on a planet of cement. The heat of the world drives people into the night; the coldness drives them to rough sex.

Now, I gather myself in a comforter and drink hot tea, watching my mother's chickens peck at the ground, watching roosters mount the hens when the mood strikes, feeling peaceful. It's peaceful here. The other planet is the rough place.

November 6

I called Sam to arrange a visit. When he didn't answer, Ma lent me her car to drive to his place in Elkins, our nearby metropolis, boasting seven thousand residents.

I squeezed her station wagon through the small streets of his neighborhood and finally up a tiny alley to reach the apartment over a garage. Old, gray steps ran up the side of the weather-beaten building, and Bob Marley music grew louder as I walked close to his door. A stolen street sign, declaring his pad Hobo Avenue, hung above his peephole.

I knocked, preparing myself for a sweaty face and red eyes.

Who's there? he yelled from inside.

Tess.

I heard feet and stepped back, only to hear him say against the door, Tess, I loved dinner, but I am biz-ee. His sharp enunciation tried to hide a slur. Hon, you knew I would be busy.

Dork, just open the door, I said, only able to see wood paneling through his peephole.

I can't reach the door, he said and laughed.

Open up, jerk.

Silence.

I pounded my fist against the door, overreacting, imagining that he'd passed out and wasn't able to find or keep a hold of the door-knob.

You're too little and scrawny to knock it down, he taunted into the door crack. Huff and puff.

Stop fucking joking, I said. An idiot, I pounded harder, bruising my pinky finger. I slammed my high-heeled shoe into the wood, making a dent. Prick! I haven't seen you in a year.

Hey, hey, he shouted. Calm down. I'm not letting you in. Girls aren't allowed.

We shouted until, worn out, I sat down and rested my cheek against the scratchy blockade. I tried to persuade him to have lunch with me. I'll drive you to your favorite diner.

Forget it, he said. You keep to yourself.

Don't be a paternalistic ass, I said. A few snowflakes dissolved on my nose and hands. Sam, let me help you.

Oh, fuck off. Stop following Ma's orders.

I dropped my head against my knees. Are you naked?

No.

Then open the door. I need to pee. It was my last idea.

Forget it, Tess.

I forfeited the battle.

Before you go, he said quietly, remember you need to move back here. Somebody in New York is stealing your eyebrows, bit by bit.

Very funny.

You looked so thin and tired. His voice pulled back. Man, watching you try to be happy at dinner wore me out. And we need you here.

I'm fine. You're drunk.

Exactly.

Sam, I have a life. And you're not gonna quit just because I'm here.

The beat of reggae floated out of the keyhole.

An ache, hot and sweet at once, pushed at the edges of my lungs. You're a dork, and I'm leaving. Bye! I held my foot above the first step for a second.

Bye, he mumbled, and I walked down to the car.

Sitting there, the heater blowing on my face, I couldn't believe he didn't let me in. I revved the engine and pulled the car away from his apartment, grazing a trashcan so it wobbled like a spinning top.

At least I tried. Ma can't glare at me anymore.

She cried though, hearing that he wouldn't let me in. She admitted that he never opens the door for her either. When needed, she pushes back the latch with a credit card to make sure he's clean, other than alcohol.

November 7

This morning, frozen grass broke beneath my rubber boots as I walked toward our mailbox where a faded scene of sledders drinking whiskey awaited the mailman and the early-morning risers. Ma used to paint a new scene for the upcoming Christmas season.

When Sam was ten, he also wanted to paint our various mailboxes, so he took the opposite side of Ma and painted a lone snowman. Then he painted a reindeer with three legs, and last came Mrs. Claus wiping her eyes with a black handkerchief. Ma didn't let him paint after that. He was thirteen and Too Old.

His next job was to help my father in the shop, sawing and sanding cutting boards while my father slowly carved harps. His cutting boards (which reeked of rebellion, according to Dad) consistently had too many angles and not enough room to slice any vegetables, except a skinny carrot. Sam quickly got booted from our father's sacred space.

He moved to collecting wood for fireplaces. Excelling in elaborate stacking techniques and in his ability to sniff out the driest sticks on the forest floor, he'd often return from his chore with flushed cheeks and the smell of sassafras on his breath. His eyes were glazed—high from too much nature, I figured.

Today, with Ma away doing house calls, I slugged from a bottle of wine in honor of Sam and sat around watching talk shows. Those poor, poor people. The audience heckled an eleven-year-old wearing Daisy Dukes: You look like a slut. Do you want to be a slut?

Her father died a year ago!

I'll fuck whoever I want, she said, whenever and wherever. Her eyes full of tears, she jabbed a finger into her chest.

Her mother wept into chubby hands, and the host, a Southerner named David Smarts, sat back in his pinstripes and let it happen.

Does he think he helps? Does he think this girl's brother will also tear her down when he walks on stage? The boy's hands trembled as he defended her. He stormed into the audience to fight the ones who said she was Rotten or a Bad Kid. You don't know us, he yelled. Fuck you. You don't know her.

When I started stripping, I called Sam. He lived at home then. We weren't talking much because of him knowing about the rape—that it happened, not who did it. I needed his reassurance.

He listened to my explanation of why (money) and how (just danc-ing), responding with, Uh-huh, got it. You gotta do what you gotta do. He advised me to carry Mace and to punch any guy who touched me.

I asked, Does it mean I'm a skank, a slut?

Hell no, he yelled, sounding like that kid on TV. Exactly the op-posite. You're making a smart living. If anyone can handle those ass-holes, it's you.

Such a relief to tell him. His acceptance kept me calm for a long time.

I've wondered, though, about my ability to handle jerks. Before the rape, I'd only slept with Zach. But then Sam watched me breeze past Rob's brutalizing. He reasoned that I'm tough.

But I miss his protection, his hot chocolate.

I should have said, If I'm so skinny, why don't you feed me? Open the door and make me lunch. Why should I be the one to fix this fam-ily? No one is that strong.

Maybe I should explain the rape to Ma and Dad.

No. They'll blame me, think I acted dumb. And Sam's right. I don't need the sympathy.

November 8: help

An attack hit me twenty minutes ago. The fear has loosened. Shit. I'm so tired. Sleep. Too stiff to lie down, my legs are still shaking. Breathe. Distract.

The purple unicorns on my lampshade are blurry. I'm fine, nor-mal. I'm not going insane. Shit, shit, shit. Where did Ma put all my old posters? Joplin, Blondie, the Bangles, all stripped down—replaced by a cream for guests. Cream, calm, cream, calm. Oh, yeah. She put the posters in the attic. Fuck, I'm still shaking.

Calming.

Ma was in the kitchen, talking about Sam.

I saw myself, a flat reflection on my mother's eyes.

I said how he's selfish.

Her eyes filled with focus, enlarging, boring into my face.

She said, He's just confused, and you've been confused too. Her sharp nose pointed down.

My stomach tightened. For a second, I thought I'd tell her about the rape after all. Wouldn't she feel stupid then, stupid and sorry for bringing up that night?

Instead I yelled, God damn it, Ma. You better not start that shit because you're lucky I didn't slap you.

Dad whispered, Tess is right. Leave the past alone.

A couple of drinks at a Thanksgiving party isn't a big deal, I yelled.

We had rules, a contract! she said. For Sam's sake.

Misty was there with me, I said. She can tell you I barely drank. But go ahead and leave, Ma. Never admit you're wrong, I shouted as she picked up her coffee, walked out on the porch, and closed the door so the click crashed through the country evening. Fights in West Virginia are loud compared to New York.

Dad patted my shoulder and followed her.

My room is less of a haze. My heart's slowing. The paper is real, the writing is real, and I'm real.

I never forgave Ma for yelling at me after the rape. And she's not over my reaction. Oh, well. Life is rough when your mother's a bitch.

She apologized at dinner, said that she hated to see her kids mad at each other. I'm okay. For tonight, I won't end up on the floor, drooling, my mind shattered.

November 9

Leaving tomorrow. This morning, Ma served me pancakes and Earl Grey tea in bed, wobbling on a tray.

I could forget. Leave New York. Diane spoke too soon when she said that I'd never feel like their little kid again. A huge part of me is a skinny girl whose mother brings her mysteries from the library. But I'm deceiving everyone now. Sam couldn't handle hearing that I work at a brothel, not that I want to talk to the asshole, but the visuals would trap him.

A man breathes heavily as he pushes and pulls a vibrator in and out. Just an image, but it reels through the mind, clatters about until I stuff so many other noises in, it becomes a tap that is calmer but won't stop.

I refused to write about this before, but a few nights, by quitting time, I had forgotten the names and faces of guys I slept with. Other girls say you lose certain guys, mainly the easy ones, the ones who say, Hi, what's your name, let's fuck, Estelle. A half-hour fuck. No problem, why even bother to remember?

Oh, I'm sick of obsessing over work. Let me write . . . about the softness of my mother's upper arms, the way she smells like vanilla. New muscles in her legs look nice, even sexy in shorts. Dad's working out with her, so no hot studs will snatch her away. An Amazon couple, carving and painting their marks on this world.

November 10

An unremarkable evening. Two unremarkable fucks.

Erin and I sat in the Lounge most of the night, watching a double feature of Bruce Willis in *Die Hard* and *Die Hard 2*. Good villains.

Everyone else visited with a girl who used to work here—a coke addict, evidently—who redecorated her entire apartment in animal prints.

And I realized that we never talk about what we do. I mean, we do, but some girls refuse to smile, cross their arms while waiting to be chosen (or rejected), and claim they hate the guys, but they don't go any further. We discuss hooking as if we're social workers with interesting cases.

Little Jim is nice, but sweats like a pig, so make sure you get on top as often as possible. Construction Pierce is an asshole, but he tips well if you scratch his balls for a long time. Swing Tony is crazy; he keeps requesting Natalie even though he doesn't have orgasms with her anymore. She confronts him with the evidence, the empty condom in the trash, and tells him to see somebody else, but he's obsessed.

We talk about details, coping—and movies.

I want new topics, new obsessions.

I wonder who I'm writing to. Myself, god (basically myself again), or maybe my descendants. My granddaughters might discover the yellowed notebook chronicling the life of their wild grandmother. Or maybe I'll accidentally leave it out someday, for my mother, father, or Sam to find.

November 12

Evening, and I'm snuggled up on my futon. Pandy's purring in the curve of my lower back. She's an enormous, furry mole on my naked skin. Susan's lounging in the living room reading a trashy novel, her red hair pulled over one shoulder, keeping me calm.

Today I walked to Battery Park. I stretched out beneath a pine tree and felt home again, for hours.

November 14

This afternoon at the community center, I told a mother that I worried about her baby spacing out, not responding to me. These symptoms can indicate early epilepsy.

The woman morphed into Crazed Mom, heaving Jesse from hip to hip, her power skirt sliding so the zipper was in the front. Lots of questions and finally, How is Jesse fed?

By herself, I said, she feeds herself, and sometimes Mrs. Davis turns her high chair to the wall so she won't be distracted from eating by the other kids. (She's a sickly, blonde child who needs to gain weight.)

The mother dropped her diaper bag on the floor and ordered me to watch Jesse, for One Minute!

I groaned and resigned myself to bouncing boring Jesse on my knees, her favorite game. She's always the last to be picked up and is constantly sick. She stares at the other kids like she'll never fit in. A weird geek at a year and a half, and she doesn't care to change.

Jesse squealed as I bounced her up and down. But when I stopped for a minute, she didn't demand more, only sat with her arms held out, looking around our room. Toys neatly packed away in big, plastic boxes, rows of crayon drawings, and the smell of Play-Doh. And we waited, not expecting anything from one another. My cousins would tear this room up, I thought and smiled.

Unfortunately, the moment ended. The director called me into the office to say that I created a big to-do because Jesse's supposed to be spoon fed, not feed herself, and certainly not facing the wall! The teacher got in trouble for not listening to the mother. And I got in trouble for not voicing my concerns in an Official Manner to the teacher (disregarding that I had already mentioned my concerns to her).

Now Mrs. Davis is going to hate me too. She already hated Jesse's mother for being overprotective.

If I'm not getting fucked in one place, I'm getting fucked in the other.

Tonight, my last customer proudly revealed his enormous dick—maybe fourteen or fifteen inches. Thank god he only wanted me to sit and masturbate, describing my fantasies.

Here's one: I dream about savagely biting off a customer's dick and chewing it into little pieces. Then I spit the bloody pieces of soft skin into the trick's face, and miraculously, while not even having a dick anymore, his body convulses in the most powerful orgasm of his life, and he has a massive stroke. The stroke instantly paralyzes him, and he lies on the bed, unable to move, his face in a smile, bleeding to death from his crotch.

I wish I'd told him that. God, it's enough I have to screw these losers; the last thing I want to do is expend my creative energy on them.

I'm in a crappy mood. I better go to bed.

November 16

I imagine leaving New York. Volunteering at the community center has been a nightmare the last two days. Mrs. Davis is definitely gunning for me.

And I'm sick of men—the Little Italy waiters who shout and whistle at me and Susan during their smoke breaks, occasionally lifting up an apron to wow us with their bulge. Sue said, You look sad these days. She's worried because I rarely leave the apartment except for work.

I moved a lot, but I still grew up in one mountain range, one forest, you know? I miss the shade of trees and porches.

I wish I knew something beyond the psychology of the sex industry.

November 17

Bored, I called home. Found out Ma's drawing again!

She was inspired by my trip home, realizing that I inherited her miniscule ears with a bumpy point at the top—fairy ears, I call them. She warmed her muscles by sketching trees that resemble our ears.

I can't believe I inspired my mother to paint. For the first time in a while, she's made me feel special.

For years, she played the Crazed Artist to the hilt, dragging us from town to town with this need for inspiration. Then she threw down her brushes about four years ago, after Sam got his DUI.

The whole family traveled to the courthouse to bail him out. We found him sitting on a wooden bench. Our feet clicked and scuffed over the marble, moving toward him. Crust had gathered in the corners of his mouth. He licked his lips the way drunks do when they're preparing to speak without slurring.

Ma sat down next to him. I dug my nails into my palm, knowing Ma would screw up, ready to stop her. She put her hand on his knee, her wrinkled knuckles smoothing with every squeeze, shaking her head. She whispered, Why? Why?

I hissed, Shut up, Ma, kicking at the floor as I swung my legs. I'd worn a T-shirt with a peace sign on the front to inspire the judge.

I remember the deserted corridor of the courthouse and a janitor smacking a lemon-scented mop near us. Dad flipped through his wallet, counting bail money. I slumped, controlling the desire to grab Sam and leave.

But Ma—Ma's case of chattering teeth soared. Why? Why? Why? She patted his shoulder, tucked his hair behind his ear. Honey, tell me why. Talk to me. Why?

And finally Sam exploded, standing up and screaming at her with spit in his words, knowing it splattered her face, probably wanting to actually spit but not having the guts. The veins in his neck. The cops turned toward us with hands on their sticks. Sam told her that she had dragged us back and forth between her hell and her misery year after year, not giving a goddamn about us, what we wanted, and how dare she judge him or wonder why he felt lost in this world. How else could he feel but lost with a mother like her, and on and on, and on and on, echoing off the cold floors, and I'm crying because he was so right in many ways, and Ma was so sorry, sitting there, eyes open, spit sprinkling her dark lashes, and what can you do once the damage is done?

I'm glad Ma's painting, but her spurt may only last a day, or until Sam self-destructs again, another seizure, another DUI. He's a ticking bomb.

Oh, my fingers are stiff from gripping my pen so tight, the way I do when I'm tired, like I'm holding onto a piece of driftwood to keep from drowning. Across the room, a crack splits the plaster near the ceiling and swells above the stereo system, turns hard behind Susan's armchair, and finally peeks out for an inch or two before slithering into the floor. A clean cut, the skin folding back, not crinkled, simply open, exposing frailty.

November 18

Whistling John stopped in tonight and picked me, the first time since the first time. I didn't orgasm. I faked it. Losing sensitivity down there. With guys rubbing my pussy like it's a rabbit foot at the racetrack, it's no wonder.

Shit, the only activity I do that requires energy output is fake coming. And smoking, I guess. But that's hardly a challenge, since I've smoked since I was twelve.

I taught Misty how to smoke on one of the first evenings we spent together.

Hollow Creek runs parallel to our road back home, and I had wanted to explore it. A week after I met Misty, I dragged her down the steep bank, my long hair snagging in the tall briers.

The crickets were out, but otherwise the air lay still. We found the creek and splashed in the shallow water. I lit one cigarette, a Marlboro Light that Sam purchased for me, and handed it to her before lighting my own. She didn't cough, just grabbed her throat and stuck out her tongue like she was choking and took another puff. Cigarettes wavering between fingers, we spread our arms and balanced on smooth rocks. The stones were cold on my soles, tender from walking barefoot for the first time that spring. Misty giggled, singing, Girls just want to have fun, girls, just want to, just want to . . .

Busy pretending to be runaways hiding our trail, I didn't notice him until we stood a foot away. Sam's head. A pool of water swirled around his neck, and his chin rested in the mud at the base of the bank. His body was submerged. Water lapped at his nose and caused him to jerk his head back unconsciously. The twitch caught my eye.

Feeling tired and old because I'd seen him like this before, I fell onto my knees, Misty next to me. I grabbed his head like a jar that I'd dropped, relieved the glass hadn't shattered. I saw a stack of beers on the shore, and Sam's hands roughly pushed at mine. As his head hit the water, the splash drenched my shirt.

He lay there, his eyes blinking.

I smacked the water's surface and yelled, Get up! Get up, Sam! I punched a few holes in the soft dirt next to his face. Sit Up Goddamnit! Get up! And he did, sloppily, his face half brown and dripping. The other cheek was white and shining in the dusk.

Chuckling, he ran his hands through his wet hair, saying, Sorry, Sis.

But I couldn't soften because then he'd make me leave him. A few unopened cans might be enough to get him to stay.

I let rage slide up my throat. I yelled, Bullshit! You're embarrassing me, and I want you out of here. I moved forward on my knees, grabbed his heavy, muddy chin, and turned it up toward the road. Are you listening? I asked loudly, but flatly, into his ear.

His eyes slipped shut.

I shook his chin, and his head wobbled like a puppet's. Cool water ran over my calves.

He coughed up a small sob. My rage drifted downstream.

His lids stayed sealed. I leaned close and sang, Walk like an Egyptian, walk like an Egyptian, oh way oh, walk like an Egyptian.

I don't know what prompted me, but Sam snickered, then snorted, his head lolling on his neck. Misty scooted back into the water, always scared of us together. A short burst of laughter shot out of me, and I stroked the dirty side of Sam's head, pulling hair out of his eyes. Standing, I lifted him with me until he pushed himself off and took a few steps.

I'll see you at home, he called over his shoulder, stumbling up the steep embankment.

Go fuck yourself, I shouted.

Probably saved his life, the crazy guy.

Whatever! I gotta stop dwelling on family because I can't do anything. Let them go, Tess. Guys who love pulling hair are the priority! Fix that.

Now, practical options: School for massage therapy? Quick and easy to earn certification in New York. I could carry on the family tradition but only help women.

November 19

I'm healed! Peter sent me a pamphlet explaining my PANIC AT-TACKS! The doctors list the most common phobias as fear of choking and going crazy. Ha! Thank you, lord!

See, instead of simply experiencing stress, I (silly old me) feel the physical components of stress and react to them with more stress—a fast heartbeat gets faster, and the throat squeezes tighter. My stress escalates until I'm reacting as if a car hit me, off balance and dazed.

In order to stop the spiral, I need to recognize the earlier stress and calm down. Distract myself by singing, humming, etc. Poof, with a magic wand!

My first freak-out, or I should say, Panic Attack, hit me after a club gig at a lesbian bar. My hands and knees shook; the whole room kind of zoomed in and out. Dehydration, we assumed. Except that after drinking water and resting, I continued shaking.

I shook for an hour while Marie and other dancers crowded around me, sipping blood-red wine and cocking their heads. I guess the non-stop stripping, acting, and rehearsing had cranked up my stress level. And earlier that day, Dad informed me of Sam's seizure.

Last night I stopped the spiral by doing the dishes and woke up Susan in the process. Good thing she likes me now.

While I lounged in the country, she missed me and has ceased prodding for brothel details. She baked me a chocolate cake with no icing as a welcome-home present—my favorite. We devoured it while running lines from *A Doll's House*. I'm encouraging her to act, channel her flair for the dramatic.

November 20

I don't want to write about the House anymore. It's all crap. And my fucking language becomes fucking obnoxious, and I see that I'm a bitter skank. However, the problem is that if I don't write about work,

I can't let the experiences go, but if I write too much, it's all-consuming.

Let's see if I can let this go: Rob told me I was a slut as he slammed his dick into the back of my throat.

And this: The night of the rape, Ma screamed at me. I had lied and told her that I fell down, but Jesus, you'd think a mother could detect the Raped Daughter vibe. I didn't mean to lie. In fact, I planned on alerting the free world, but walking in our house was . . . surreal.

The fireplace burned as Ma and Dad snuggled on the couch watching TV. A glass bowl sat on the coffee table, popcorn kernels in the bottom like pebbles in a fish tank. The burnt, buttery smell rushed at me; nausea dug at my throat. Our cat Smoke slept on Dad's lap. Tigger's soft belly arched upward, his paws raised in the air, letting Ma scratch his chest, and the house was so warm. Hot even, and I'd just been naked in the snow with a knife to my throat. I wasn't ready to register the heat or Ma or Dad. I couldn't get a step away from the battering cold.

A mistake. Ma and Dad freaked over my tripping excuse, the first stupid reason I thought of. But the look in my eyes, the blood around the corners of my mouth, my ripped shirt—they should've guessed. They should have guessed.

I never pursued it, you know. Our mothers go to the Unitarian Church together. Ma and Ellen feed the homeless side by side, spiritual sisters. What am I supposed to do with that? Destroy that dream?

Ma loves her bubble of acceptance, a yearning she finally caved to when she sought comfort because of Sam's drinking. Ma's mother, Grandma Mary, rigidly enforced all that normalcy stuff, keeping up appearances. A drill sergeant about table manners and cleanliness. She smacked our fingers for reaching for the salt shaker at our own table, even Dad's hand. Took pride in the plastic trails on her rugs that led from one room to another.

Before one of her visits, Ma scrubbed the house from top to bottom, even climbed a ladder to clean the windows. She moved the television into the attic and watched me and Sam like a hawk for unruly behavior, whispered at me to change my clothes because I smelled like a Cheap Smoker (the only time she acknowledged my poorly kept secret). And Grandma Mary would nod approvingly at us but still criticize Ma for wearing jeans or adding too much spice to our food. That must have sucked.

Ma said that Grandma was trying to make up for her husband taking off when Ma was little. A single mother in the '40s was watched carefully in her small town.

When Grandma Mary wasn't around, Ma usually resented the pressure to be perfect and rebelled, but the tendency was always there. She'd say, Sam, settle down (before someone sees you). And, Tess, keep yourself in line (because one embarrassing child is enough). Hard to fight against the habits that parents drill into you.

November 21

I saw a few guys, including City Gary. He's a tender man. But, as ridiculous as it sounds, I'm pissed that he screwed another hooker while I was in West Virginia.

He says he's falling in love with me. What the hell?

I like spending time with the asshole. He makes his fingers trip and fall over my nipples. He kisses and rubs the back of my neck, says how smooth it is. How my shoulder blades look like angel wings.

He brought me a silver ankle bracelet with linking stars and moons.

Yet, apparently, this adoration doesn't restrain him from screwing other girls.

Whatever! Time to change the topic!

Presently, Susan is walking around naked. Beautiful girl. Small breasts, thick legs, and one of the roundest butts ever, all topped by red hair to the middle of her back. Her body type never tones, carries baby fat that creates flawless skin.

I once made out with Marie. Never again. No arousal. She's a bad kisser, lots of teeth. At the time, I assumed the kiss sucked because she was a girl, but then Tente confessed that Marie practically knocked out his molars too. Anyway, if I hooked up with a girl again, Susan would be my first choice.

I bounced up and down on her bed a few days ago, explaining my Panic Attacks. Her response? She stared at me and announced that I needed to see a therapist.

I curled in front of her. Pulled at her arms until we spooned. Honey, I said, you could chew off a therapist's ear. I wiggled around to face her. You're a Fatal Attraction waiting to happen, I said. Calling your ex-boyfriend and hanging up. Tut-tut.

She whispered, You use sex to control guys and your fear. Sliding an eyebrow up her forehead, she dared me to argue.

You're right, I said. I'm proactive!

Whatever, she said and pinched my ass, demanding that I make her breakfast. So I did.

I like our place. Kind of an odd mix. I contributed the worn, black, leather couch. She owns the navy armchair. Her bedroom is oak furniture and framed posters of Degas dancers; mine is decorated with ripped-out magazine photos and scarves pinned up with thumbtacks, reminders of a gypsy childhood.

I suddenly am remembering Sam walking out of my closet and laughing until tears filled his eyes the April Fool's when he moved all of his toys, his decorations, and even his bedspread into my room as I slept. My look of utter bewilderment and then embarrassment kept him in stitches for weeks.

November 23

Susan does high-end temp work, so she can take off whenever she's financially set. This week, she's set, so we've Done Brunch the last couple of days. We joke and talk about clothes and celebrities until our brains drip out of our ears.

I dragged her to my favorite drugstore on Fourteenth Street and Avenue A. We perused the nonperishable-food aisle and walked away with Cracker Jacks and Fruit Roll-Ups. We each bought a box of sponges (the kind that prevent pregnancy and periods) to plug our vaginas any time we please. A sale blew away our good sense, and we purchased twenty different nail polishes between the two of us.

I've decided, partly inspired by Susan, that I'm quitting the community center. Beth has branched out, loving other teachers. And though it reveals that I am a petty bitch, I'm jealous. Mrs. Davis has been hostile since the Feeding Debacle. And the subway ride to the Upper West Side is not worth the headache. And really . . . what metaphor can I use? I am a wart on a beautiful woman's face. I don't belong and might be spreading cancer.

In my other life, not a single guy chose me tonight, for the first time ever. Yes, this pussy finally had an evening to relax, trick free. I watched TV.

But, don't judge. My life is not a waste! I juggle many responsibilities. I vigilantly lotion my body to keep a sweet smell exuding from my pores. I had my mustache waxed yesterday—the only problem with Italian ancestors. Afterward, feeling like a plucked chicken, I kept touching my lip, even when a cute guy jogged past me on Twelfth Street. I also trim my pubic hair regularly before it grows too long and gets in the way. Then I conscientiously apply gobs of conditioner to prevent freshly cut hairs from poking guys. Busy, busy.

Gary and Susan barely grow body hair. They're smooth like Native Americans. I'll think about their bodies before I close my eyes. My bedtime snack.

November 25

I talked to Peter this afternoon—the annoying motherfucker. And he lectured me again, this time for saying that Hasidic Jews are nasty and perverted. Well, he is Jewish, but hardly orthodox, so I didn't think he'd be so touchy.

I know that I describe the tricks as Nifty Types (to quote Peter) that fit into Neat Boxes. But the clients ARE easy to simplify because they always request the same shit.

What breeds this? You're warned about the specifics of a guy—how long he likes to go down, if you should whisper the whole time, whatever—and, by god, it never fails that the guy requests or acts out those exact behaviors. You literally could be any-fucking-body. Tricks want their ritual—their PB & J hooker—the one they have every day for lunch.

And, to be honest, different ethnic groups do act differently with the girls. Asian guys tend to be good lovers. Hasidic Jews are nasty. Arabs are smelly. But no black guy has picked me yet, so I'm no authority there. Listen, I'll admit they're individuals, but the hell if I can keep everyone's complexity in mind, particularly when MY fucking complexity is never acknowledged . . . And guess what? Tonight a nasty Hasidic Jew wanted me to suck my thumb while I sat on the toilet! And I forgot to tell him that I was on my period, plugged with a sponge, so technically, he sinned his ass off in more ways than one.

Women, when you bleed, do you ever want the chunks of skin to be bigger?

November 26

Got off the phone with Misty. I called her to chat, and she wants me to read *The Tao of Pooh*. Ay-yai-yai! I'm not certain of anything these days, except that *The Tao of Pooh* wouldn't help.

Our conversation was brief. She wanted to discuss when I'd quit the House, but I refused to speculate.

She lectured me for acting so tough, refusing to back down.

From who? I asked, and she didn't have an answer.

I used to shake her out of Miss Mature mode. As gawky fourteen-year-olds, we used to skinny-dip in Blue Hole and stuff river sand down the back of each other's bikini bottoms. She'd bring bread and her parents' wine, and I took charge of cheese and candy bars, for a perfect picnic. We frolicked—that is, until the boys made their appearance. Then she stopped playing, focusing instead on thrusting out her small breasts.

Susan is my new role model. I love how she fully enjoys her food, compared to how I only eat for sustenance. For brunch, she orders one pancake with strawberries, three sausages, bacon, scrambled eggs, a fruit dish, and a side of cottage cheese. To drink, she needs coffee, orange juice, water, and a glass of milk. She carefully twists her hair back into a knot and leans over, slipping a morsel of each item onto the prongs of her fork.

Our brunches last a good two hours, and we leave huge tips. We analyze problems the waitress with the tattooed face will encounter if she ever leaves New York, if fishnets are actually cool, and why David Letterman is better than Jay Leno.

November 27

Before I left the community center today, I gave notice. Mrs. Davis stared at me.

I said, Okay?

She rolled her eyes.

I blew a hot breath at my bangs and moved to grab my bag. Midstride, my shoulder smacked hers and knocked her back a few feet. Pain shot through my socket.

Worrying that I broke the bone, I rolled the arm again and again and again.

At home, I climbed into my bed, sang and rocked, and watched the news. I wasn't able to calm down for hours. My teeth chattered. My hands remained cold and sweaty between my knees.

I want to be rescued. I want Ma to hold me, Sam to tickle me, or Dad to read me to sleep.

November 28

This morning, I moped, only venturing out of the apartment for a couple pizza slices. I ate them bundled under my comforter, my high heels still on.

Midafternoon, I woke up to Susan's hair tickling my face as she shook her head back and forth above me, grinning. Tea and a bagel in hand. Reaching up, I cupped her cheeks and kissed her coffee-tinged lips. She slipped under the blankets with me and ate half my bagel while I complained about the brothel and Mrs. Davis.

She rubbed my shoulder.

I liked it too much. Noticed her nipples poking through her blouse. Soft legs pressing against my thigh. Musky perfume seeped into the tips of my fingers.

I'm hot, she said, throwing back the comforter. She chided me for sleeping in my clothes.

Too tired to undress, I said. I should get up.

No, she said, you need to relax. She leaned over to unbuckle my heels, throwing them onto the floor. I watched her full butt, her tight jeans. She hooked her fingers under my tights and pulled them down, staring at my legs. Then she lay on her stomach again, this time her face above mine, her eyes on my mouth. Her tongue skimmed the inside of my lips.

I returned the favor. She caught my tongue with hers and began sucking on it, gently. But after a few minutes, I wavered. We continued kissing.

Her fingers slithered under the waist of my panties. I tensed. I had no desire to go down on her.

I stopped.

She wasn't sad or pissed. She smiled. What did you think? she asked.

Nice.

She leaned in for another kiss.

I pulled back, slipping into a double chin.

She dropped her head and laughed into my shirt, her breath against my collarbone. She said, You're such a flaming heterosexual, it's no wonder you can fuck all those guys.

My mouth dropped open.

I didn't mean it like that.

Like what? I said.

Oh, for god's sake.

I slammed back against my pillows.

Straddling my hips, she ranted about how I analyze and admire women's bodies. I made her curious. Turned her on. She had thought we might Get Wicked. But I definitely get it, she said—you're weirded out, and I'm kind of heated up. Shit, Tess, I've fucked lots of guys. I don't judge. It's just that being a hooker is wild, yet you're put off by a bit of girl-on-girl. It's funny. Get mad, hit me, but don't get all distant.

I lay there, staring at my parents' photograph next to my bed— Dad's lips pressed to Ma's cheek, her eyes lowered with a slight smile.

I grabbed Susan and pulled her into a serious noogy, rubbing her head with my knuckles while she squealed. Next time, I yelled, talk to me first! And you're right! I don't want to make out again. I let her go and pushed her away with my elbow, not too hard, sticking out my tongue.

She shoved me back. Fine, but I'm the best kisser you'll ever meet.

You wish. I pushed out my butt, pressing her toward the edge of the bed, until her feet hit the floor, and she dove, grabbing and chewing on my bare toes.

That girl is so crazy. Maybe crazier than me. I love her. I'd normally brood over the deeper meaning, but what the hell. We both found out what we wanted to know. We're cool. The only depressing thing is that I didn't enjoy it much. It burst my fantasy bubble, filled with Susan and me escaping New York for a cozy igloo in Alaska, adopting children and puppies.

November 29

I walked over to Chinatown's public park for the first time. It's five blocks from my apartment, but I'd never been. Inside the metal fence, I passed a Chinese woman hunched on a crate, advertising palm readings. I followed a wide, curving walkway to the center of the square where a crowd of old Chinese men swarmed around card tables. A dozen Chinese women stood on the outskirts, and me.

I leaned against a tree and watched. Clicking echoed in the low-hanging branches. Retirees in cheap suits sat at the tables, holding sticks of white and black ivory, the shape of dominoes. They placed four of five of them in a row and then lodged them between the tips of their fingers and the tops of their palms.

Turning up their palms, they'd quickly look at them without letting the other players peek, and then they'd smack them back onto the table. At that point, the players exchanged pieces, knocking the bars against each other, clicking together another neat row, and scooping them up to look again, and so on. The players didn't speak much, but the men standing around them spoke nonstop, watching.

I drank my pop, noticing some of the men looking at me hard, puffing on cigars, leaning on canes. Pairs spoke Chinese and watched me until I felt more than uncomfortable. I got annoyed.

This is my neighborhood too. They must expect tourists with the palm readings, I figured . . . but no white people visited on a weekday, in the middle of the afternoon. They're betting, I realized.

But I don't look like a cop in my fake fur coat. My orange wrap-around dress doesn't exactly scream Police.

I tried to stand my ground as a neighborhood local. They know me at Excellent Malaysian Food, I wanted to shout, but I ended up sulking out of the park, feeling guilty for intruding on the Chinese home away from home.

I don't know what I'm doing in New York. Watching old men play mah-jongg?

I just might move back to West Virginia like Sam suggested.

November 30

Dad called.

Around midnight, as I cuddled City Gary at the House, dreaming about moving home, Sam drove home from his favorite bar, The Shop. He swerved down the construction-lined highway, his station wagon sliding back and forth on the black pavement like a needle on the end of a record. A huge blinking arrow thrust out into the road, commanding him to merge with the right lane. Unable to make out which direction it pointed, Sam turned the wheel to one side, then the other, and smashed directly into the sign, slinging glass everywhere. His windshield exploded, cutting his lips and cheeks, and collapsed into his lap. The visor slashed open his forehead. Luckily, he did avoid electrocution, missing the major electrical box that ran behind the sign.

He blacked out before other drivers found him, blood trickling down his face, not noble enough to fall unconscious from the blow, only from the alcohol. One small boy saw Sam and went into hysterics. His parents want Sam to pay for therapy.

So, goodbye to Big Brother's license for at least a year or two (hallelujah!). His car is totaled anyway. Also, this means the asshole will serve time, probably more than the minimum of forty-five days, maybe a whole year because of the gravity of the accident and it being his second DUI. The trial is scheduled for March 1. Then the fines, the attorney fees, etc.

Shit. Dad and Ma better move into the Al-Anon building.

December 1995

December 2

The phone rang as I walked through the door after a quiet lunch at Excellent Malaysian Food. Dad was on the other end, doing the usual: How's the weather?

He said, I really miss you, Tess. I heard him scratching his beard. And I choked up. Pandy paced in front of me, and I told Dad that the next time I visit, I'll bring her to kill all the mice and snakes because she's tougher than their lazy cats. And we both laughed ridiculous belly laughs. He said that he and Ma talked. They'd love to see me move back in with them so that everybody could support each other.

I don't know, I told him.

He sucked his teeth and said, I'd figured as much, but Ma misses you. No real pressure, but I know that you ground Sam, and Sam needs help. If you don't have anything to say, he said, don't say anything. So I didn't. We discussed kitty litter for a few more minutes and hung up.

Susan thinks I shouldn't go, particularly after Ma left her own melodramatic message on the machine, saying that Sam almost died. We'll pay for the ticket. Would it KILL you to visit again?

Made me want to kill her, kill Sam.

The night of the rape, the bathroom door opened. Wearing only my bra, I sat on the toilet seat, my legs spread. Red wads of toilet paper lay on the floor, my thighs and stomach streaked with blood. And Sam stared, his eyelids weighted with hot moonshine, his chest half in, half out of the door.

Just a little rape, I said and laughed, tears dripping off my lashes. I threw a piece of toilet paper down and crossed my hands over my vagina, still stinging, oozing. I said, I don't think I'll tell the parents, okay?

And he hunched there, his flannel shirt hanging from his body like a cape, staring at the blood on the tops of my feet. Really? he whispered.

Don't worry, I said and pointed to a towel hanging out of my reach.

He reached in the door and tossed it to me.

Just forget it ever happened, I said, placing the towel over my lap. They don't need to know.

Who . . . ?

Next time give me a ride home, huh?

All right, okay, he said, pulling the door toward him. I'm sorry, sorry. His voice leaked in through the closing gap. The door clicked shut. And I missed him the moment he left me there.

Never did a fucking thing. He never said another word.

I'm playing a Tom Waits CD. He soothes me. I love his deep, raspy voice, his depressing take on love.

December 3

Diane gave me crap about my face breaking out.

What's wrong with you? she said. Your skin was clear a week ago.

I think my pimples are a good thing because I'll definitely repulse Rob if I ever see him in Elkins. I'm just dying to move home. According to Ma, Rob visits his parents all the time.

Hey there, skinny guy, I'd say. You impressed me that night. You know I block the details, but I do recall that you came twice, right? So strong and healthy. I've taken, like, ten AIDS tests, and they've all been negative!

At home, I'd enjoy walking with Sam hand in hand (because Ma won't come) to his AA meetings where drunks sit nervously in dark corners of the church basement, smoking, twitching in metal folding chairs, and refusing to acknowledge my presence. I loved it at sixteen, seventeen. I'm sure I'll love it now.

December 4

I yelled at Ma for pressuring me to fly home again. No, No, No! And I hung up.

Then I asked Susan if I should tell my parents about Rob raping me, so that my fury might ease, so that I could forgive them for not understanding. Sipping coffee at the Blue Moon Café, Sue answered, Secrets are what make us individuals.

I looked at her laugh lines hidden under thick foundation and the red lipstick pasting on fuller lips.

Susan, I said, secrets or no secrets, we'd still be individuals.

You're too romantic. A confession won't cure your family, cure the alcoholism.

But Susan doesn't understand the details. When I walked in the door that night and saw the strange world of comfort, I meant to scream, Kill Rob, but I stopped.

I didn't even know I had bruises on my face.

So when Ma and Dad stood in front of me, touching my cheeks and asking questions about what had happened, I jolted. Listen, not a big deal, I said. I got a little tipsy and tripped.

What? You were drinking, Tess? Ma pressed her hands to her belly.

Ma, I only had a couple drinks. Their faces faded out of focus as I imagined Rob crashing through the front door behind me with a semiautomatic, killing us all.

Listen, I said. I need to lie down.

You signed a contract, Tess! Mom said. We all agreed not to drink around Sam.

Dad reached out, his forearm brushing my face, and squeezed my shoulder. Tess . . . you look drunk. Did Sam have anything to do with this?

I stepped back. Blood slipped further down my thighs. I grabbed the sides of my head. You guys! I said. I cannot handle this. Just please, get out of my way. And I ran to my room.

I locked my windows, closed the blinds, and pushed back the clothes in the closet to see if Rob was crouched there, smiling at me. I threw open every drawer of my bureau. Down on my scraped knees, I squinted into the darkness under the bed. I jerked back at Smoke's form, shaking as I swept my arm back and forth in the corners I couldn't see. I checked my closet again, kicking the back wall. I tested the window, slamming my palms up against the wooden frame to make sure the locks worked. I threw back the covers of my bed, lifted up the pillows. I wanted to call Misty to warn her about his threat, but if I stopped watching my window, he'd appear behind me.

So I lay on my mattress, stiff. Throbbing crotch, breasts, mouth, and throat. Images of Rob breaking my window, stabbing me in the chest, lowering in a gun and blowing out the side of my head, shoving the barrel up my vagina while I slept.

Ma came bursting in, Dad behind.

Ma said, Jesus Christ, Tess, you know how we feel about this. It's enough we have Sam, but now you—you, too! We will not tolerate this behavior!

Dad held out a placating hand. You know your mother feels strongly about this.

I looked back and forth at each of them and pulled my blankets up to my neck. I said, I only had one drink. I tripped is all. I wasn't even tipsy, honestly.

You said you had two drinks, and why lie about being tipsy? Ma asked, her eyes huge and black.

I don't know, I said. It just popped in my head as an excuse for falling instead of just being a stupid tripper. I tried to laugh, my throat stinging. Now, come on, I said, leave me alone; I'm exhausted. I tasted blood as I swallowed, and I smelled Rob. I smelled the sweat of his crotch on my face, even in my hair, as I turned into my pillow.

Have you looked at yourself? You look drunk, Ma said. You look like you've been rolling in the goddamn grass, drunk. Tripping is not an adequate explanation.

And I freaked.

I couldn't help it. Ma's lips were tight as if I'd been beating up old ladies, and Dad looked crushed. I was disgusted, enraged. Couldn't they even see my ripped shirt? What was wrong with my fucking parents?

I screamed, Fuck you. Get the fuck away from me! Who the fuck do you think you are? You don't understand shit, and you never have. It was you forever. And now it's Sam, Sam, Sam. Fine. But don't you dare walk in on my life. Don't you dare!

Dad said, Now, honey.

Ma yelled, Shut up, Tess! This isn't helping!

So, I rushed at them, shoving hard at Ma's chest, Dad's shoulder, over and over, out of my room.

Then Ma screamed in my face, Stop it!

I screamed back, reached up and grabbed her face with my hand. I squished her mouth into a raisin, my fingers digging into her closed eyes, and shoved her backward with all the force of my body. And Dad caught her as she fell.

Don't you ever, ever come in here again! I slammed the door in their faces, my kitten poster flapping in the puff of air, scaring me because I thought Rob was flying at me from behind the door.

Silence shook the house for a day, except for my late-night talk with Sam and a panicked morning call to Misty to see How She Was Doing, not telling her because I worried her guilt might break us or since she and Rob were old friends, she might not believe me. Because of details that would have to be recounted, too grotesque and humiliating to face.

And then I headed back to school.

So angry. I still am, but I'm mainly sad. Basically, I feel forgiveness. I frightened them, and people react to fear without thinking—at least my parents do.

Sometimes, they still startle at my voice. They look scared of Sam, too. I guess that's what happens. You love your kids, and one day, those kids realize you've screwed them up in one way or another, and you sense the anger.

I want to enjoy New York again. To forget.

Slipping into denial, I'm joining Susan in front of the boob tube.

December 5

Gary returned tonight. Rolling around on the canopy bed, we chuckled about him and his buddies sky diving. They transform into Macho Guys when they hit the airplane, using the lingo, arm-wrestling, patting asses. He brought me flowers and asked me to call him at work, promising that he'd whisk me away from Manhattan.

His sister is a recovering cocaine addict, and her roller coaster almost destroyed his parents' marriage, so he respected my anger. He pointed out that if my parents took Al-Anon seriously and allowed Sam's mistakes to be his own, they wouldn't ask me to fly home, to drop my life.

Not to be totally perverse, but Gary reminds me of Sam—long limbs, dry humor, earnest, and confident of my adoration, prone to covering his gaping hole of insecurity with a twisted grin. I understand him. He's also more socially adept, ambitious, and upbeat. And, most important, he's not an alcoholic.

We're not supposed to see customers outside of work. Diane calls it stealing, but I'm scheduling one date, testing our potential.

Other news: The community center is replacing me with a part-timer who's already there, so my two weeks are no longer necessary. Today's your last day, Mrs. Davis said and tried to brush past me, to bump my shoulder, but I darted out of the way.

When she announced, Miss Tess won't be coming back, sweet Simon looked up from draping a scarf over his skyscraper, stared, and returned to work. Michael hugged me but was distracted by the art supplies set on the table. Beth stayed home sick today. And Jesse didn't glance away from the TV. Kids can break your heart.

Oh, well, they're tough from growing up in Manhattan. Know better than to grow attached to a flighty thing like me.

But, here in this place of peace, I'll whisper how sad I am never to see the kids again. (Sad, sad, sad.) Okay, now I'll move on.

No one to talk to because Susan's out on a date with a guy she met in acting class. I forgot to mention that she's officially acting.

And now, I need to find direction. Resolutions for December:

1) Control my panic attacks.
2) Date a nice boy.
3) Consider waxing my bikini line.
4) Engage in activities outside of the House and writing.
5) Call Gary.
6) Fall in love.

December 6

I CALLED HIM! I called Gary at the advertising agency. And he acted like a Smooth Operator who'd gotten his way. I love arrogant men. My stomach's tight and squirmy. The truth is I like him and life is short. He wants to meet me for dinner. OH MY GOD, WHAT AM I GOING TO WEAR? I'm calling Susan at work to ask her. I'm too hyper to write, except that he said, I almost fainted when I heard your voice.

What a line.

Later: The blow-by-blow is that I've called a cab to take me to Delilah's in the East Village. I picked the restaurant at Gary's insistence—isn't he sweet? I'm wearing my faux fur, which I hope he doesn't think is tacky. Jesus, I sound ridiculous. I'm sporting my dominatrix, high-heeled boots; a long, wool skirt; and a tight, shiny top. I look gooood! I'm happy to be happy. (I also applied lots of mascara but only a dab of lipstick in anticipation of first base.)

There's the cab! Bye!

Much later and sleepier: I met him for dinner, and it's ten thirty now.

The night began with Gary's rant, detailing how the Other Woman, Roxanne, confessed to her boyfriend, which is how his wife found out about the cheating. He said that he never loved his wife in the first place. She was just a fuck-buddy, and, at thirty, he thought he should marry. Wants to kick Roxanne out of his house, but she refuses to listen. He took a bite of his steak and imitated the way she eats her food, slow and circular, like a cow chewing its cud.

Kind of funny, but I admit to forced smiles over wine teeth. He seemed distant clothed, wearing a silk suit and alarming tassels on his dress shoes.

He bikes every weekend to escape her. And supposedly, they sleep in separate beds. He leaned close and puckered up his face, saying that he wants her to—poof!—disappear.

I stared, realizing that Drunk Gary can be a bore.

He blinked, sat back. Sorry for going on about my problems, he said and thrust out his hand, palm down, for me to slap, to punish him for being a bad date.

Not necessary, I said.

I want to be punished, he said, with mock seriousness, flapping his hand at me. Punish me.

No.

Please?

If you put it like that . . . And I smacked his hand hard, cracked it with my fingers.

Ow! He grinned and then had me kiss it to make it all better.

After dinner, we French-kissed down sidewalks. We played the Couple People Love to Hate by making out in the bar. Girls gawked at me squirming on his lap, and men walked by, smiling but not saying a word 'cause this BIG guy is feeling me up and making me laugh by smacking my ass now and then. In the end, I wrote my phone number on a napkin and tucked it in his suit pocket.

It's fun to get jittery. I like dating, showing a man off in public, him showing me off. I need a nugget of gold in my life, even if it is fool's gold.

I picture myself as a feisty wife of an old coot I still find handsome and funny. I imagine myself cooing over grandchildren before I envision my own babies. The thing is, I want a happy ending. I don't mind the means, but grant me a sweet end to make life worth the heartache. And this guy is sweet enough.

I caught a cab home, and he gave me fifty dollars for the ride, thanking me for a special night. He apologized again for talking too much.

I figure, better that he spew his insecurities today so he can relax next time.

December 7

Gary called me from his work this afternoon—Yes, it's time to examine another stool sample of Tess Ruscello.

Strange call. I hated laughing at the secretarial demands that inter-rupted us and caused me to morph into the patient daughter/sister. But Gary appeared to enjoy the chaos. He's the bigwig executive, so what can little old me do but wait.

Anyway, anyway, the reason I'm depressed is self-indulgent and stupid: he's busy tonight! So, I'll flop around, watch TV, read bad women's magazines, and listen to foul foreign language shouted on the street below while he hits the town with his buddies.

Do I sound totally obnoxious? Yes. Doesn't the fact that I refuse to act on these stupid tantrums count for something? Yes. And the next two nights, I'm hooking, so no dates for the next three days! It's not like I love him, but . . . but . . . I WANT HIM TO DISTRACT ME! Gary, please drive me out of Manhattan like you promised, lay me on a bed of grass, and kiss me all afternoon.

I'm restless. I feel stifled already, only one date into the relation-ship. I hate the fact he's living with a girl and dating me. Sam and Ma made me powerless. Their moods and needs controlled our house-hold, and this waiting, waiting, waiting triggers my stupid combina-tion of passivity, impatience, and anger. I need to communicate or I'll dump him like I dumped the others.

I'm going to buy cigarettes, a whole carton.

December 8

I suspect that Gary didn't call today because he's upset that I didn't put out. Obsessing over a self-centered trick is absurd, but I hate it that he'd hold my no-sex-on-the-first-date stance against me.

I just wanted to feel like a normal girl for once, one who doesn't screw the moment I'm alone with a guy who may rape me anyway; I figure we might as well screw, so I can stop worrying.

With Rick (my last un-paid-for lay), there was no attraction, but I figured kissing might ignite a spark. One thing led to another, and we ended up naked.

In my boarding room at 3:00 a.m., bored and exhausted, I wanted to chill out, but he was still excited after an hour of foreplay. He massaged my butt, kissed my neck, and cut me off every time I tried to get in a word.

Rick, I wonder—

Oh, I plan on sucking your lips for hours.

Well, it is three—

The night is ours.

I'm not sure—

I brought protection, you worrywart.

I gave up.

Yes, sir, it takes effort to get into my pants. No wonder Gary's disappointed.

And another thing, Gary shows bad father potential. Though totally dysfunctional, my parents act better than Mr. Distracted, Mr. Put-Out, Mr. Me-Me-Me.

Yes, Dad takes too much personal space, but he enjoys hearing others speak. Gary rolled his eyes when the waitress told us the specials, like she intentionally dominated the conversation.

I admit that no matter where we lived, Dad barred humans under thirty from his woodshops. As kids, we actually painted No Fun Allowed on his shop doors, and he didn't blink, simply nodded and locked himself in for lunch.

But once, when we were packing for the move from Charleston to Elkins, I snuck into his shed to hide. Escaped the scene on the front porch, where Ma screamed at Sam for not helping the movers. She was angry because he'd flunked all his college classes. These big guys in overalls watched and spit chew on the ground, jumping forward when Ma punched Sam on the side of his head. He ignored her. Dad must've heard the yelling at the house when he arrived home.

I heard him trudge up the gravel driveway to the woodshop. He paused inside the door for a moment, scanning the room littered with piles of white pine and cherry boards, carved harps waiting to be strung, sawhorses and a rocking chair for whittling. I thought he probably smelled the smoke from my cigarette. His black hair was a charred nest above his head, backlit by the white skin of sky. I crouched lower behind the old doors stacked against the wall.

After a period of shallow breaths, I peered out and saw his head bent, heard the circular saw roaring to life. His huge fan blew the sweet smell of cut wood into every corner.

I hid there for an hour, listening to him hammer and drill, and watched as he put on his goggles. Sometimes an arm came into view. He'd walk close, and I'd see his shiny dress shoes covered with sawdust. He flipped on the radio and turned to pop music. A miracle, I thought—my dad listens to music besides jazz! I swayed, ignoring the slats of wood pressing into my spine, my fingers drawing chubby animals in the sawdust.

And finally Sam came, shouting in the keyhole that dinner was in ten minutes. I sat up, watching Dad prepare to leave, putting his equipment away. His feet passed by, headed to the door.

Tess, he said, turning.

I fell back against the wall with a thud.

Tessy, what's waiting on the sawhorses is for you. All right? Go take it to the moving truck. Go on now. It's good to have a hiding place.

Hearing the door creak shut, I pulled my smashed cigarettes from underneath me. Loving Dad so much for knowing I needed to stay, loving him for his silence and the noise of his tools. Loving him for the music and no lectures about smoking.

I crawled out. The shed door was open a crack, sunshine streaking across the floor. And, on the sawhorses, there sat an enormous wooden box with big, silver screws holding it steady. Knots covered the white pine. The lid had a hook-and-eye lock on the inside.

I circled my hideaway, pushing long, dirty hair out of my face.

Hearing another dinner call, I quickly hauled the box down, staggering from the weight. I dragged it toward the light, plowing through the sawdust, leaving white marks on the cement floor. And before anyone could say boo, I leapt in. Stayed long enough to see the line of sun trace itself down one wall.

My hand swung into the end of the beam, and I cupped gold in my palm.

December 9

Refusing to mope any longer, I called Gary this morning. He's helping his mother paint her basement, so he can't visit me at the House. Bastard. And Susan spends every minute with the new actor-boyfriend.

Hard to be a hooker, alienated from the rest of the world. (I'm also naturally a self-centered slut, but that's beside the point.) However, my red lightbulb should cheer me shortly.

One of my happiest memories is my sixteenth Halloween, right after I began dating my first (and only) love, Zach. A popular senior, he admired my fearlessness in class and guessed that I'd appreciate his secret love of Kafka.

I was stunned when he asked me out the fall of my junior year, knowing, as everyone did, that my brother was a drunk and that I attended AA meetings with him.

We hiked the Blackwater Canyon together, not talking much, just kissing a lot. We drove his three younger brothers around town. Watching their Little League games, we'd hold hands. And he ran to the vending machine to buy me Cokes and Snickers.

I attended cool-kid parties with him. That year, shedding my boxers and T-shirts for my new boyfriend, I celebrated Halloween as a skinny Carmen Miranda, my long hair pinned up, wearing a hat covered in plastic fruit. I sewed a lining to the inside of my black skirt, and the red silk peeked out through a high slit. In the high-school gym, I salsa danced by myself, watching Zach as he watched me and pretended to suck on his corncob pipe, sexy in his ratty overalls.

We slipped outside to drink beer and smoke pot.

He'd taken my virginity the week before, with slight pain and definite pleasure. So we walked to his house. We crawled through his bedroom window, collapsing onto the floor.

He kissed me deep and hard until I pulled back and whispered, I'm scared of having sex again not on the pill.

Okay, he murmured and rolled flat, and I followed. His heavy hand pressed my head onto his thudding chest. And he stroked my neck.

Cherished. I felt cherished.

I barely knew him. We barely talked. I didn't know him when I clipped his fingernails on the soft bathroom mat. And I didn't know

97

him when I broke it off the week before his graduation because of a passing notion that he didn't take the relationship seriously, which boiled down to a teenage boy and teenage girl not knowing how to talk.

I wanted to share, communicate, scream, but I couldn't pry open my mouth after years of silence. (I had shut up because Someone needed to hold it together while everyone else fell apart.)

I hear he's engaged, living somewhere in Texas. Lucky girl.

I continue to lose the bravery that I once liked about myself, so I don't think about Zach often. But maybe I'm learning from us, finally.

December 10

Sam called me earlier, though we only spoke for a few minutes before he had to leave for work, washing dishes at a new place called Dino's.

He coughed and apologized for not opening his apartment door when I visited. Said that he brooded for the last month, feeling guilty (over that, but he didn't mention the traumatized kid at the car crash). Asked me if I was pissed.

I reassured him that I'd forgotten, because I dislike discussing his alcoholism and mean streak.

I asked him about his trashy girlfriend (I always forget her name), prompting him to describe the bad photographs that she took of him while he slept.

He wakes up to find her shooting a 35mm as she gallops across the room in her cowboy boots—to capture his blurry essence, she claimed. He said that he's blowing her off for being too needy, wanting his approval, wanting him to show the photos to Ma. Everybody thinks they're an artist.

He advised me against dating, to focus on my acting goals.

Whatever. I'm unmoved by Sam's apology. I miss hiding in my golden box.

I miss—Summertime . . . when the livin' is easy . . . fish are jumpin' and the ramps are high . . .

I'm peeling off my apricot facial mask, lying on the couch, and watching Tom Brokaw delve into Eva Perón's psychology, whose mind lab-coats have dissected and labeled on graphs with neon arrows. My thoughts turn to subway smells and Italian ice.

I'm watching a streetlight melt the winter's first snow on its silver crown.

Eva Perón. Rumored to have been raped by aristocratic young men, which drove her to the city where she stripped and thrived.

I move like mud in this city of slumping bodies. The cushioned barstool, when it notices my weight, sighs, and bears my legs wrapped around its metal neck, a woman's fear of chaos.

I miss the softness of dirt and wood.

December 11

Gary came to see me at the House. He surprised me with a benevolent smile and a leather necklace, a blue feather hanging from the middle.

Who am I? Pocahontas?

Why do guys always buy me simple gifts? Other girls are wooed with gold and diamonds, and I receive a string of leather. Do men think I'm stupid or deep?

Let's not kid ourselves, Gary. Don't deny your commitment issues. If you're attempting to financially lure me, step up to the mat!

During our hour and a half, the jerk massaged my back, thighs, calves, breasts, temples, and neck, only agreeing to enter me after I convinced him that sex was a form of pampering.

He told me about his mother, a widow, locked in her house, praying for the angel of death to take her, to reunite her with an abusive husband. He cried. I wiped his tears.

He said that women had always saved his life. He said, Women do so much, take so much, they ought to be cherished.

So, of course, I love the leather necklace. And realize I'm an over-sensitive freak.

December 12

I am a WOMAN—A BIG BAD WOMAN. I'm gonna refer to myself as Wonder Woman from now on—no more plain Estelle. Hi, I'm your hooker for the evening and my name is WONDER WOMAN.

This afternoon, before an incredibly busy night, I was walking down Fourteenth Street to do some shopping when this Hispanic guy, standing in the door of a Laundromat, spotted me walking toward him. He and a friend were about fifty feet up the sidewalk, and I picked up my pace, high heels clicking and scratching against the cement. Twenty feet from them, I focused my eyes on a baby carriage coming from the opposite direction, and this Hispanic guy started whistling.

My heel hit a crack, and I yanked it free, barely a pause in my stride. Hey, baby, baby, baby, he called to me, and the muscle between my shoulder blades cramped.

I put on a disgusted face, which he must have seen as I swerved and swooshed past his wiry body.

Still tense, I charged ahead, waiting for a tight hand to grab my hair and yank me back. Instead I heard, Hey you, Doll Face, I want to eat your pussy. Can I eat your cunt, honeypot?

I took two more steps and stopped. And, without thinking, with the baby carriage upon me, I turned around and dropped to the ground. I plunked my purse to the side, propped my hands behind me, and spread my legs.

Thank god, I exclaimed. Thank god, I repeated. I've been waiting for this moment. Would you . . . would you please eat me out? I am so horny that I leave wet spots on chairs. Would you lick up the extra juice, please?

He stared, shocked for a second, and started laughing with his buddy, telling him that I was crazy in Spanish. Hey, I said louder. Motherfucker, I told you to eat my pussy!

He looked at his friend and then back at me, his laugh getting forced.

A harsh tone worked into my voice. Come on you piece of shit, little dick . . . pussy! LICK MY CUNT! Breathing fast, jerking my legs wildly to emphasize each word. FUCK FACE! Hurry up!

And now he wasn't laughing, and now I wouldn't stop screaming, and the woman turned her baby carriage around and left, and the men shot me dirty looks and retreated. And I was alone, the cool air of Fourteenth Street lifting the skirt and lightly blowing on my panties.

December 13

It's 4:00 a.m., and snow balances on street signs. The neighborhood glows. I stood on the sidewalk, my lashes catching the flakes. Peacefulness after a peaceful night at work.

Only Gary came in. He wanted to know why I hadn't called him yesterday—so sad. Busy Christmas shopping, I said and laughed off his serious face.

He ended up talking about how his wife threatened to fight the divorce unless he met her for dinner. Before the food arrived, she cried and begged him to seek therapy, to love her again.

Straddling him, I shook his shoulders and said, You have to get tough! Let me call her.

He hugged me, smelling like Irish Spring soap. I need you to protect me out there, he said.

I said, You're right.

Then we discussed career options. I write a bit, I told him, and he thought it suited me. As he left, he said I was clever and slipped me a hundred-dollar tip. I want another date soon, he whispered. You're too precious to slip through my fingers.

Keep it in perspective, I said to myself.

I'm not sleepy, so I'll walk back into this smoky night. Walk down to the deli and purchase milk for morning coffee. Or I might catch a cab to the closest twenty-four-hour drugstore—for a bounty of hair ties, eyebrow pluckers, bubble gum, and lip gloss.

December 14

I found Susan a leather miniskirt with a cowgirl fringe. I dug through six used-clothing stores. Sassy, sexy, and funky. She'll love it.

I bought Dad a flute. Engravings of dancing figures swarm over the wood. He loves carving—it's his true love, more than literature, though you'd think that god struck down those who didn't memorize the St. Crispen's Day speech by the way he beat Shakespeare into our heads.

I loved reading HIS plays, PARTICULARLY "All's Well That Ends Well," but I only latched onto acting in high school. Gliding over the stage as Blanche, I crumbled under Stanley's knowing. All dressed up in a southern accent. The heat of stage lights passed for Louisiana suffocation, and water replaced alcohol. I reacted to every beat of dialogue, action. And the applause of students and parents gratified the life I'd lived those two hours.

I craved that full-bodied experience. Three weekend performances created an addiction.

I rejected the sheltered world of NYU because of the rape. Felt too easy. But sometimes I think if they allowed freshmen to perform onstage, to lose themselves in the backdrops, protected by the fourth wall—well then, I might have stayed.

I suppose stripping became my recurring role, my escape. YES, I guess so.

Goodnight Susan, who's snoring because she caught a cold. Christmas is near.

December 15

I came and came until I walked like a bow-legged cowboy. Yep, Gary galloped back into work as he promised. And we booked another date to hear a lounge singer.

Most cool—I quietly explained that I didn't like his wife being in the picture and Roxanne living with him. I repeated what Susan keeps saying to me: I deserve someone who's all mine.

He slid down and softly kissed the mound of my vagina, saying, You're right. You don't need this. I'll work it out. I'll find a way.

Maybe I can teach him to be consistently attentive, to grow a backbone.

I saw another client with a waxed mustache. He sells oriental rugs and wanted me to lick circles on his belly. I felt like a product-free window washer.

December 16

At the House, a Christmas tree stands in the Living Room, tinsel on the handrails, and the girls wind down the staircases wearing elf hats that Janice made. A long version of "Winter Wonderland" pipes into the rooms, which is a bit disconcerting compared to the usual elevator jazz. Mistletoe hangs above every bed, and we offer the gentlemen spiked eggnog as they arrive.

And people think hookers' lives are hard and no fun!

A lot of guys dropped in tonight. I made a bunch of bucks. We're like mailmen—it's assumed we need a holiday bonus, which we do, we do.

I woke Susan with a wet kiss on her cheek. She smiled and snuggled deeper beneath her blankets. She's still dating the crazy guy from her acting class, though last night she said she doesn't like him much. He's all competitive since their acting teacher began to sing her praises.

December 18

Well, it's the morning after Gary and I attended the concert. I'm sitting in the kitchen alone, relieved, drinking tea and having a smoke.

Over dinner, Gary barely smiled at my story about Pandy puking in the shower and me accusing Sue of the nasty deed. He said, I've never owned pets.

I tried to tell him about the rug seller who wanted me to wash his stomach with my tongue. I joked that I could be an environmentally friendly window washer, but that tensed him up. We're both growing possessive.

Gloomy date overall. We drove to The Club, this huge room with couches and a stage at one end. Early on, a DJ played music, and I danced by myself, which I love.

I roll through my waist, hitting beats with my hips like a belly dancer, shrugging my shoulders in hip-hop form, boogying out; I need space. A few guys that I planned to ignore moved closer when Gary rose and plunked himself next to me, rocking from foot to foot, his hands suddenly on my waist. I turned my back to him, shimmying my hips. He rubbed my neck. If I turned toward him, he locked his hands behind me and leaned in for a kiss. I kept flipping to get away. No luck. In the end, I blew off my annoyance because I understood—he's attracted and territorial. But the night continued.

We took a taxi back to my place, and the event was noticeably less thrilling than screwing at the brothel.

Doesn't that suck? Isn't that shitty? I didn't even orgasm. I faked one, though I normally have multiple with him.

With the bedside light glaring in my eyes and no background music to focus on, I kept asking, How ya doing? He'd whisper back, Just fine, and go totally silent. He usually grunts and moans the whole time.

JUST FINE! Huh?

Shit, after he licked for a good half hour, I wanted to move on, so I suggested that he Insert Himself. He responded with, Just a bit longer—I love your taste, and ate me out for another twenty minutes. Sweat dripped from beneath his blond hair. He never sweats! A huge pool of liquid spread under my butt. His saliva, not my juices. Moans of boredom flowed from me.

He requested that I finish him off with a blowjob—almost impossible because of his enormous penis. I yearned for a mint-flavored condom. I don't want to taste salty pre-cum or tinges of leftover urine, or slide my tongue over a potentially infected penile opening. I want dimmer lights to cover the dark shadows under my eyes, to hide upper-lip pimples from my mustache waxing. Let's go back to the brothel where bedroom lights burn low like candles.

Right after we finished, he scooted off the bed and wanted to shower (a first). It was three o'clock in the morning and neither one of us could sleep, so we watched TV in our towels and drank beer until Susan arrived home and demanded that we go to bed.

Anyway—whine, whine. I don't know if it was him or me. He definitely acted nervous.

Last, but not least . . . I panicked in the middle of the night. I hummed in the dark, staring at the white ceiling, running my fingers through the tassels of a shawl hanging next to my bed. Thank god he didn't wake up. I hummed "Puff the Magic Dragon" to fight off fear. I pictured him smashing the lamp over my head while I slept.

I'm sore from arching my neck, pressing my forehead against the cool wall, while the rest of me stretched against his back, like a stupid turtle. I was afraid to pull away—the flood of air might wake him.

I used him as an excuse not to talk to Ma when she called an hour ago. She did manage to slip in that Sam is already sneaking drinks. I refuse, however, to dwell.

Once, a brief fling and I went to this quiet spot in Central Park and made love. The secrecy thrilled me. Mr. Rebel, he wore kilts. Brown hair in a braid. I sat on his lap, like they did in that movie *Braveheart*, and nobody could tell. We'd stop pumping when someone walked by, and then begin again.

My shirt hung open, my breasts bared—I pressed tight against him so no one saw. He sang and thrust to a rhythm, making me laugh. If I had a hammer, he sang, I'd hammer in the morning, I'd hammer in the evening . . . ! One of my favorite sexual encounters. We lasted about three weeks, until we made love in private. Yes, I see a pattern emerging.

December 19

I hung out with Susan today. Attended her acting class. A blonde went first, performing with . . . unparalleled spontaneity? The chick literally made her upper lip quiver. Lady Macbeth as a rabid dog.

Susan and I grinned and kicked each other under the metal folding chairs.

A black curtain draped across the back wall, and this queen in jeans and a tank top hefted the heavy drape so it muffled her face, wailing, Out Damn Spot! Then she bowed, flushed and so proud.

That performance increased my admiration for the truth that Susan brought to Stella, living in the Louisiana heat, tackling her thick hair with bobby pins, using a handkerchief to wipe her armpits. She made you resent Blanche's artifice, even while you knew Stanley's attack loomed.

When I played Blanche, the audience rooted for me because I played her as a fallen angel, a moth, a fragile creature. Susan's forwardness, her life by instinct, makes her Stella, and me—I'm too agonized to be Stella and really too tough to be Blanche.

Afterward, Susan wound her arms around me, asking, Did you like it? What did you think?

And I admitted that she did an incredible job, that she was a natural actress.

She smiled and said, Yes, I think so too.

Maybe I'll find work at a theater. Not acting but gluing costumes and nailing together stage sets. I'd bathe in the camaraderie while avoiding roles.

Marie and I used to earn extra cash with club-dancing gigs. To prepare, we'd hot-glue sequined prom dresses onto cardboard pieces to create headdresses. My crown was a pot leaf, which meant I didn't dance as much as I slinked on top of this small stage with hundreds of kids bobbing in a swarm below. The music so loud, the vibrating floor forced me to hit a beat. Drunks hung off the balcony, calling to friends, screaming at us. Marie, as cocaine, wore a white leotard, silver sequins, and a big, fake razorblade on her head. The razor suited her stiff body. The type of girl who goes crazy when they're stoned because they secretly fight a prudish nature.

I'd peer through the fake fog and see her far across the room dancing like an Egyptian, her face deadpan as she stuck one hand in front of her chin, the razor wobbling.

She hasn't called me since heading to California. I'll take her hint that she's moved on, and I should too.

Time to move on. Yes, I gotta quit hooking.

Though on days off, I miss the companionship, all of us on our toes, able to anticipate the different tricks, figure out how to please them. I get the urge to visit if I don't work for a couple of nights. My ultimate distraction, my final theater.

Soon, I promise myself and my sweet pussy that I will stop.

December 20

Sam woke me up around 1:00 p.m. to say that I didn't need to rush home for him, as if I'd been packing my bags since the crash.

While pouring myself a glass of water, I lied and said that I'd considered it but didn't think I could help. I said that compared to family chaos, the city seemed restful.

He said that he's fine. Smoking lots and slowly dumping his girlfriend. Taking out the trash, he calls it.

He joked, I can't ask the beautiful girl to wait for me while I'm in jail.

I asked him how his cuts had healed.

Like superhero wounds, he said. They've vanished. We're all good.

Really? You sound tired or something, I said, crawling back under the covers with the cordless.

He laughed for no reason except to cover his ass. He said, I concentrate on staying calm. You see, life is not meant to be fought against.

I closed my eyes, listening to him convince himself that this attitude is productive. Don't do shit, basically. He's consistent, that's for sure. (My thighs and stomach streaked with blood and he walks away.)

I interrupted his philosophizing with, I'm so happy to hear you're perfectly fine. I'm fucking fine too. I'm so happy. What a brother I got. Lucky me!

A pause.

Well, now, that's the spirit! he said. That's my girl! I want you on my team! Red rover, red rover, send Tessy over!

You're wacko, I said, rolling my eyes. You have no idea how fucked up my thing is, so don't give any pep talks.

You're awesome, he said.

You have no fucking idea!

I have the coolest sister in the world, and I love her!

You're an idiot.

I love you, he said proudly.

Okay, okay, asshole.

I love you.

Fine! I laughed. I love you too, but I gotta go.

After we hung up, I cried. He pulls this every time. Charms, cajoles, but he never stops. He never stops drinking. He never asks about my tough times. He loves me, but what good are abstractions?

Then I shook him off. ME, ME, ME. I need to focus on my goals.

December 21

My final shopping spree is about to commence.

What to buy Sam? Music? A nose-hair clipper would serve him well. A vacuum for his hellhole . . . ? I'd love to find a muzzle—slow down both his drinking and charm. A get-out-of-jail-free card? Decisions, decisions.

Now, for Ma, I've already bought all the books on cooking and alcoholism. She probably needs paint. With effort, I might gain access to special brushes, allowing her to draw a life with no children. A tongue clamp to keep the nasty lashing at bay. Though hard to mail, the sensitive way to go might be a broom to fly.

Too many ideas.

Later: I finished my Christmas shopping. Though not exactly life-altering, I decided Ma needed quality paintbrushes from this art-supply store. For Sam I bought guitar strings and a book called *The Secret Pact of Robert Johnson*. Peter is receiving a beautiful CD of *La Bohème* and cinnamon sticks.

I bought Misty a silk scarf and a bottle claiming to be Love Potion. I will give her the gift of my forgiveness as well. I decided that her college experience should be all-encompassing. A messed-up, old friend is too distracting, so I'll let her be.

Being incredibly efficient, I also wrapped and mailed my gifts, spending a bag of money on overnight express shipping. Overall, I'm pleased.

Of course, now that Sue's invited me to spend Christmas at her parents', I'll need to buy generic presents for them. Good. I need another project.

This is Big Mama, three-five-niner. Over and out, Big Daddy World.

December 22

I'm exhausted after a dreary night of work. Even now, as the flakes flutter past the bars on our windows, I swear they're sighing, tired of falling. How can I stand the ritual? Time and again. In and out of rooms. I barely do prep work anymore because nothing surprises me.

Always the cold, ceramic toilet under my stocking-covered foot as I hike up my skirt to apply a dab of lubricant.

The bathrooms are my safe box, the silent rooms in the House. Heat pours out of vents along the baseboards, soothing with a steady hiss.

I thought of the snowflakes all night. I wondered if they're relieved by the pavement's warmth—how sweetly their bodies release into the wet concrete and lose shape. I wonder if they prefer this to landing and quietly waiting on top of others, not able to see soles pounding toward them, tires rolling. Perhaps they feel the vibrations, anticipate the blows, whose suddenness won't hurt as much as shock them.

Dissolving sounds like the wise choice. Do other people wonder how snowflakes feel? Or consider a prostitute in New York?

My thoughts ramble in the bathroom.

Every night, I sit on the toilet and pull up my satin thong, which I've learned to wear on top of the garter belt. In one corner, the bathroom mirror is blurred and spotted by dried water. I lick my thumb and rub in circles, squeaking. A woman's laugh seeps through the walls; a man's follows, louder, headed toward the exit. I push aside the white trash bag, looking for spares underneath—Sarah never stocks supplies. Sometimes, I hear a radio turn on where the man waits naked. I lift the metal can of Lysol spray from beneath the sink and drown my residual smoke in a glittery haze.

I hear him coughing.

I wash my hands, carefully scraping my nails over the bar of soap, white, clumpy moons gathering at the edge of my fingertips. And I rinse, rolling one hand in the other under bubbled water.

I dry my hands on a towel and press it to my stomach before tossing it in the wicker laundry basket.

Finally, I put my hand on the doorknob and hesitate, knowing better, but imagining that I hear a mattress bouncing up and down. But like the man, it quietly waits for me.

December 23

Work slowed tonight. I saw one man—the one who asks girls to live with him for free room and board in exchange for housework. That's all I ask, he says. I don't want nothing in exchange.

He's a weird redneck, looks like somebody from home—mullet, wearing cowboy boots. His hands so rough. We get his kind occasionally, and I wonder where they sprout up. Long Island? He goes on about the big loft that he wants to share in exchange for simple companionship, and blah blah blah.

And while he talked, I gave him a hand-job. My fingers were tired, and a funk (general crotch odor) rose. My stomach started to churn. I stared at his face, searching for beads of sweat, a tightening jaw, or a mustache twitch, clues to indicate he was near climax.

The kicker—when I slowed down (because of my fascination with his weird behavior: discreetly picking his nose while a woman pulled on his penis)—this guy reached down and patted my hand.

The second time I paused, he cocked his head in warning and snapped his fingers against my wrist.

Call me the bad-reception radio! Go ahead, sir, give her a whack, and she'll get back on the right station.

And finally, finally, after prepping myself to speak up and tell him we needed a new technique—out of nowhere (he was literally in mid-sentence about a plumbing disaster)—whoosh! His dick convulsed. And I shoved the tip away from me, like adjusting a joystick to keep Pac-Man from the ghosts.

This guy . . . I wish I'd spoken up. Guys always get away with pinching my nipples too hard, fingering me like they're digging for gold, pulling at my pussy lips. Once I walk into the room, it's like I'm obligated to cooperate because I agreed to this; they pay good money, so I gotta be the Good Hooker.

This redneck scared me for a second, like the one who dragged his fingers through my hair. You're killing me, killing me. That one.

No, you asshole. You are killing me! You are drilling holes in my mind.

I need to speak up. And not just in this clear space of paper.

December 24

You'll never guess who came in: Gary.

And you'll never guess why I agreed to see him: after blowing a wad on presents, I needed the money. I'm pathetic, eh?

After the deed, Mr. MIA said that he'd missed me and . . . loved me (yeah right!). He apologized for not calling, explaining that Roxanne's move into her own place had interrupted his plans. But wouldn't I come over tonight?

I thought about my Christmas shopping for loved ones. I compared my hours of work with his trite trinkets and lack of calls.

Concluding that he doesn't care for me the way I would care for him, I pressed my lips together in remorse. I placed my hand on his shoulder and said, I need to be alone. I'm sorry, I can't date. I'm not ready for a relationship.

Then I lied. I said, I'm no good for you.

And yet, because I'm a greedy bitch, I generously offered to let him book sessions with me in the future, in case the goodbye-forever seemed too dramatic. He gave me a hundred-dollar tip.

I'm an asshole. Now he'll keep crawling back in hopes of more dates.

Oh frigging well. He has probably dealt with his PB & J hooker before anyway. Let him live the fantasy through to its destruction; I'm concentrating on me.

I talked to my family earlier. They put me on the speakerphone and opened my presents while I listened.

Ma choked up over the paintbrushes. Sam thought the Robert Johnson book rocked. Dad played a song on the flute.

I miss the smell of the Christmas tree and the fights over how much tinsel to drape. I miss the fireplace flushing our cheeks. I miss stockings with candy canes and coal.

Yes, I'm a single woman alone in Manhattan with a cat and ice cream.

December 25

I'm in Sue's parents' guestroom. An enormous suburban house. I'm a bit uncomfortable with the clean perfection, glinting carpet and shiny marble to draw the eye away from life's messiness. Their room-by-room decorating (a romantic bedroom, a hypermodern study, etc.) reminds me of the brothel, without the edge.

Regardless, opening presents and singing carols made us all giddy. Her dad won't be home until tomorrow because of business, so we just ate leftover Halloween candy with her mom, Jackie. And Sue hooted over the leather miniskirt, so I'm pitching a no-hitter this year.

I gave Jackie generic chocolates; she gave me generic bath stuff. Reminds me of Susan, with her red hair and no-nonsense attitude, but she's all ambition, advising both of us to get graduate degrees. She kept saying, You're both so smart, and with the opportunities you have as women today . . . She wore a red power suit when we first met, and later she traded that for casual workout clothes: a blue zip-up sweatshirt with matching flared pants.

Jackie owns a uniform for every occasion, Sue said.

December 26

I think Sue's dad might have been a trick of mine. When Sue went to the bathroom, he asked if we had met, said I looked familiar. This after he teased us over breakfast about dating like we were fifteen-year-olds who hung out at the mall.

I want to run away.

But I'm not certain! I'm pretty sure I've met him and can't imagine where else. Unfortunately, nothing stands out about him to really remember. He's a fifty-five-year-old guy with short, brown hair who wears a suit. He's stocky but in pretty good shape, enough to carry himself with confidence. His features are average, his wit is average. Seems like a nice workaholic.

I think he's been staring at me, but even if he has seen me at the House, I doubt if he'd be able to put two and two together.

Christ, suburbia is probably a hotbed of tricks. Bored, bored, bored. No, I can't believe he was a trick. It's just his eerie average quality—the way he watches the sports channels while reading the paper, the way he was thrilled to receive cufflinks for Christmas, the way he asks his daughter to Help Your Dad Find His Slippers—that reminds me of the johns. The factory line of businessmen that file in and out of my bed. NEXT!

And this afternoon, touring the local mall, Susan and I located the average, bored people our age who wear chain-store jeans and work at offices nearby. They spend Friday night eating at Chi-Chi's, loading up on margaritas. Afterward, they stumble through the mall's music stores, head for the listening booths to hear the newest CDs on hamburger-bun earphones, and exchange high fives.

The local radio DJ sold raffle tickets and sucked in his beer gut to hit on the thirteen-year-old girls. I held Sue's hand as we wandered, entranced and jealous of the contentment I sensed.

At one point, Sue left me to pee. Alone to gawk at the crowds, I sat down on a bench, and this kid with porcupine hair sat down next to me and asked where I lived. A cute, dorky teenager wearing high-top sneakers. I leaned over to him, my black tights stretching thin beneath my fuzzy, blue miniskirt. I smelled his sickly sweet cologne. A laugh erupted from my chest, and I said, Honey, I'm a prostitute. Don't waste your time.

Yeah right, he said, huffing out a laugh.

It's true, I said and tucked my chin down to look like a second-grade teacher.

Whoa, he said. He looked me up and down. His shy, admiring attitude shifted.

No, I stated. I am not on duty, and I'm too expensive for you, so run along now. Go hunt for girls in your league. I waved my hand near his face and looked past a herd of girls for Sue.

As he sauntered away, he mumbled, Bitch, his head tilted back so I heard. Asshole average people.

December 27

I worked tonight, naturally. Kept worrying about Sue's dad showing up! Thank god for the video monitors, and I still think I was just being paranoid.

I work tomorrow too, but I have New Year's Eve off, so me and my sweet roommate are gonna rock this town. She bought me this awesome hat—an enormous, pink ball of fluff. With eyeliner; frosted, pink lipstick; and my dark hair hanging down, I'll define *fabulous*. Of course I can't wear my new hat to work.

Diane got mad at me for wearing a leopard-print miniskirt and leather boots.

Diane yelled, Hey, go-go dancer, come over here.

I ran upstairs, saying, Stop being irritated with me, Diane. I bring in money. Anyway, I yelled, girls who work for catering companies aren't as bland as us.

December 28

I called Gary, returning the three scary messages that greeted me yesterday after work. In each message, he said, I miss you so much and want to see you.

I panicked, noting no mention of my refusal to date him anymore. Called him to clarify the situation.

At first, he chattily described his Christmas Eve in a cold bar and asked me what I'd done.

I told him that I'd traveled out of town.

I want to hear all about it, he said. When do you want to meet?

Suddenly, I'm stressed, wanting to call the stalkers hotline. I don't know my schedule yet, I said, so I'll call you later at your place.

He paused and admitted that Roxanne had moved back in. Evidently her new place fell through. And I realized that she never moved out. She also had traveled during the holidays.

He began describing how she monitors the caller ID. My head throbbed, feeling sorry for the woman.

I sighed and dropped back onto my bed, scooting until I found the pillow. I remembered how he reminded me of Sam. But he's Sam without the guilt. All the sensitivity of self, but no sensitivity toward others.

Never mind, I said.

What?

You don't get to keep me and continue fucking your mistress. You're probably still fucking your wife.

It's a fluke that she moved back, he said. I want to be with you.

Well then, I said, I won't accept the exhausting push and pull anymore. I sat up slightly and slipped my voice into the tight, high tone of a psychotic girlfriend. You want me, I said, and I want you too, so . . . let's move in together.

He laughed. You're kidding.

I'm dead serious, I pounced, intent on scaring the hell out of him, heave-hoeing him out of my presence for the long term. I referred to a nice piece of property in West Virginia. We need to move to the country, I said. We need to commit ourselves to a healthy life. Gary, you say you want to take care of me.

Silence.

I rolled onto my stomach. Come on, talk to me.

You're joking.

Why are my needs a joke when they don't line up with yours?

It's too soon.

Do you want me or not?

Tess, the chance you're offering is overwhelming, but I'm considering. Can't we wait a while? You might like New York with me. Remember, this is where raw energy feeds. We'll date more. I don't want to rush you into anything. You're so young. He let out a whoosh of air, a pencil tapping near the phone.

But I make up for my age in experience, I said. I don't want to date. I want to get married. People work out lonely shit in the fringes. Building a relationship, we'll need peace. Don't pretend you never plan on marrying again, that you never want kids.

But the divorce isn't even final. Roxanne needs me, my place, right now. Let's just date a lot.

I honed in for the kill. I pulled up my shoulders and clamped the phone to my ear. Forget it! I shouted, serious now. I am not Jane fucking Eyre. I don't sit on my ass waiting for a man to grow the fuck up. I sat up, exhilarated. I've tolerated your wishy-washy attitude long enough. Fuck you for leading me on! You're either ready to leave Roxanne and your wife, or you'll never see me again. You've got thirty seconds.

And I knew he'd never agree to leave his precious city for the sticks. I knew it. We softly breathed into the mouthpieces. I watched the clock, the second hand shaking into each slot.

Thirty seconds—I hung up. Passive aggressive motherfucker.

I'm smiling. Gary's out of my life by his own hand. FREEDOM.

And yet, Pandy's in heat. She's drooling and dragging her stomach on the floor. Her black tail twitches high in the air, begging for a little release. And I sympathize.

December 29

For once, I truly wanted a john to pick me and not one looked my way. I'm a bit worn from drinking yesterday, but damn. What am I?

Chopped liver? So I volunteered for tomorrow. I need to make money before the holiday season dries up.

After I spoke to Gary on the phone, Sue and I drank shots at a new bar on Tenth Street. Then we danced together the way that bored, exhibitionist girls do at quiet bars with no dance floors. I surprised myself by talking to a nice advertising flunky working his way up the ladder. Blue eyes and black hair. They don't grow 'em cuter. He wanted my number.

I eventually relented to his charm and wrote my digits on a piece of paper, regretting the decision as Sue and I walked outside. I paced the icy sidewalk, shaking my hands loosely from my wrists to ease the tight emptiness inside, struck with a sudden absence of self, like the floor dropped out from beneath me. I hummed and paced until Sue asked if she could help.

Yes, I said, pointing at the bar. Run back and tell him that I'm a recovering heroin addict who is moving home. Cry and say that I deeply regret my mixed message, but a man might distract me from my recovery.

And the cute man understood. He wished me the best and gave my number back.

Sue said I'm crazy, but she also put her arm around my shoulders as we walked home.

My longing for romance scares me. Before I try again, I must evolve! Find a direction or learn to handle the one I'm speeding down. Gary's failure (along with my list of men before him) proves that I'm incapable of selecting good men at this time.

On that note, I've also retired my silk nightgowns, sensing that I won't meet a soul mate in my bed and that the flannel pj's my mother sent are more comfortable. One problem: the cat falls asleep on my back while I write, pressing me down on the buttons. Large, pink circles run up and down my stomach, like military ringworm. I tease Sue, rubbing her with my strange belly, pretending to infect her with my disease.

December 30

Tonight was a thick swim in the shit sea.

A customer fucked me like we were porno stars. Lots of raunchy foreplay. The actual intercourse was even grand until he started barking softly, pretending to growl. I turned and saw him pant with his tongue out. It wasn't over the top, but he still managed to turn me off.

However, I can't exactly say, Not in the mood for the dog routine tonight.

So, I figured he'd be done soon, no big deal. But minutes passed, and he still pumped strong, panting, growling, and I started drying up. My walls began to tug with each thrust.

I moaned, as if building to a climax, even shuddered a fake orgasm, but my pseudo arousal only encouraged him to shout, Yeah, baby.

Rough. The sticky condom stretched. And the skin on my palms, scraping against the rug, scattered shots of pain under my skin. I took short breaths and squeezed, so he wouldn't be able to slide as deep. I inhaled, ready to scream—mouth open wide . . .

He pulled out, sucking in breaths like he was about to sneeze, then yanked off the condom and came in his hand.

Reaching down to check my vagina, my fingers returned blood-free. Excusing myself, I literally crawled to the bathroom where I found a red, sore area next to one of my lips, but no blood. No blood, only raw skin. I scheduled tomorrow off. It'll heal.

I sat on the toilet seat. Red marks from the rug speckled my knees and palms. My fingers shook as I smoked, holding myself gently with a cupped palm. I never dried up at the brothel before. My body always works on autopilot, with a bit of lubricant to help. I figured I must be a natural: my body must need this much sex.

But for a second there, I saw myself so cold and stiff in the woods, my insides tearing. I floated above and quietly watched Rob. I watched and thought my body might explode like a wine glass when a note grows too high and hard.

Diane reluctantly gave me permission to leave early.

A panic attack is growing inside of me, tremors running from between my legs.

December 31

Killing time while Sue breaks up with Actor Boy. So evil, on New Year's Eve. She wants to be memorable. What a freak.

Hey, guess what I did earlier? A chin-up! I eyed the shower-curtain rod. Grabbing the metal, I locked my grasp and slowly lifted my body, wiggling my toes until my chin grazed the bar. And I thought I'd lost my tone. Yahoo! I am a powerhouse. A partying power girl, wearing the purple boa that Sam sent and Sue's pink hat. I'm shooting for the Sexy Clown, my favorite look.

Pandy's fixed. She's lying around, her pink belly skin shaved and exposed. I mistakenly let her out of the cage when we got home, and she wove around the apartment, knocking into table legs and falling over. She's back in her prison, so I can concentrate on other things and ignore my guilty conscience.

My vagina looks better, but I also don't want to dwell on that. It'll snap me out of my chipper mood.

All right, Sue's back. Gotta go. We're club-hopping after Peter arrives!

January 1996

January 1

It is officially the New Year, folks. We partied hard last night. Peter met us at the apartment for shots. He also supplied weed—a lovely drug, if I must say so. Then we staggered from one steamy bar to another, only slightly shaken into sobriety by the icy winds that clawed down the streets.

We stopped at Jackie 60's, where a crowd of handsome boys and drag queens wowed us, where the music kicked harder than at other clubs. Queens ran back and forth on this tiny stage. A fake sex-change operation (all mimed as the music pumped) was underway. Actors sawed an enormous dildo off this guy's underwear. The guy lay on a surgical table and kept kissing his fake tits as he wailed in supposed pain. A nurse paraded the skewered penis while the doctor pushed his nose under his/her skirt. The crowd loved it. I loved it.

Before we left, a queen dressed as the New Year, wearing a banner and carrying a torch, vamped down the catwalk. Next thing you know, Peter was standing in front of her with his tongue sticking out, eyes rolling, his head swinging side to side as the New Year pretended to give it to him from behind. I clapped, screamed, and jumped up and down—until I slipped and grabbed a hold of a dyke's jacket, dragging her onto the sticky floor with me, both of us laughing.

The rest of the evening, we wreaked havoc. Sue and I grinding, dancing together. Dumping the Actor Boy set her reckless mood. She made out with numerous boys, until her face was permanently flushed from smeared lipstick. This led to a handful of phone numbers, which we sorted on the table, trying to connect slips of paper with faces.

Tension only rose when a middle-aged Suit approached me. I was drunk, so I just stared at him for a few minutes while he droned on, his hand sticking to my sweaty back.

And finally (well, later Sue told me what I said), I shouted, Hey, hey! What are you thinking? Do you think a gorgeous, intelligent, young woman like me would be interested in an old fuck like you?

I patted him on the chest, doubling over in laughter.

He started walking away, but I called him back, Say, wait, no wait! Why would prime pussy want a withered dick? Come on, talk to me! Make me understand! Peter and Sue caught the management staring and dragged me away.

All I remember is his hand on my back. But I'm proud I challenged him.

And here's a little ditty I just learned from Erin, who just got a book of dirty limericks for Christmas:

> There once was a woman from Kanass
> Whose tits were made out of brass.
> In stormy weather, she'd clack them together,
> And lightning shot out of her ass.

January 2

It's 4:30 a.m., and Sue traveled to Jersey again. My insomnia is incurable if she's not in the next room, but I calm down once the sun is up, so I'm staying awake until sunrise.

Turns out barking-dog man filed a complaint about me locking myself in the bathroom for the last fifteen minutes of our session.

Diane heaved herself out of the recliner and jabbed me with a finger. Cool it, she said. Remember who's paying.

Luckily, she lectured me while other girls hung around the basement. Janice says that she's not truly angry if she deals with you in public.

After me, Diane took it up a notch and screamed at Erin for not showing up to work last week, calling her a fat, lazy slut. Erin turned into molasses, morphed into a nonresponsive blob on the couch. Diane smacked her upside the head a few times, hair flying out, hard enough to hurt but light enough to brush off if you wanted.

Erin apologized, monotone, under her breath and said that she'd work extra this week. Looked like she might kill Diane.

Shit, Erin said afterward, rolling and then smoking her own cigarette, spitting out the loose tobacco ('cause she's that cool). Ma is twice her size, and I used to take her out. Erin grabbed a throw pillow and bit down on a corner.

She said, I'd grab hold of her blubber and sink some teeth in. I only kept quiet, Erin claimed, because if I'd spoken my piece, we would've gotten physical fast.

She said that I shouldn't sweat my lecture either. Never made easier money, is her line. She calmed me.

Nothing else to report. I cranked up the thermostat but am unable to shake the winter chill. Luckily, Pandy's warmth is slowly spreading. My butt and thigh muscles ache, weak from dancing.

But I'm regaining my nutrients from Ma's fruitcake. Sue's appalled, but I more than like it—I love it! I defiantly love fruitcake!

January 3

In a moment of Christmas spirit, I called Misty. I caught her at home as she headed out the door to a movie. Breathlessly throwing on her coat, she said that she saw Sam and Ma in the Food Lion stocking Sam's fridge. Thank god the cart wasn't loaded with alcohol, she joked. She'd also heard about Sam's DUI. Maybe jail time is For The Best, she said.

I remained polite and let her excuse herself. Screw her naïveté and her subtle judgments.

With Sue's encouragement, I called Sam afterward. He was absorbed in computer solitaire. Come visit me, I said, before you head off to the big house.

He dropped his Mr. Cool act.

That's a good idea, he said. I would need to save up a little money from the new job. And I bet the parents might chip in. Maybe I could even treat you to a Broadway show.

Bus tickets are cheap, I said.

I gotta check with the cops to see if leaving town is okay.

I'd take off work and show you around, take you to my old daycare to meet an awesome girl named Beth. We'd order pizzas and eat Italian ice.

Get a couple of cheap tattoos!

I groaned. But, I said, you can't drink before or you bleed too much.

Me drink? Wrong brother.

If you come, will you take it easy?

Sure, sure. I only drink when I'm bored.

Yeah, right, I said. Visit soon, before my birthday—February 14, in case you've forgotten.

Is being twenty-one going to make you less of a smartass?

I doubt it, I said and signed off.

I want a mildly sober brother to try out different diners with me, to analyze the thickness of bread in a grilled cheese, the spices in chili, the acid in orange juice. We'd bond, away from the parents. I know it's a long shot, but I'm hoping.

January 4

I saw Swing Tony tonight, Natalie's regular, who she refuses to service anymore. He's an old guy who fakes coming and looks like Sherlock Holmes—a big mustache that twitches as he rushes to the bathroom with an empty condom under his tweed jacket, destroying the clue. He talked about her the whole time, asking me if I'd wear her perfume next time, and was I sure Natalie wasn't around?

I was tempted to turn up his hearing aid and yell, SHE'S NOT HERE, DUMBASS! Instead, I murmured, Honey, all pussies feel the same, so crawl in and pretend I'm your girl. A pussy is a pussy is a pussy.

And it worked. Well, at least he got off. I think.

Afterward, he kept calling me Young Lady, thanking me for a nice time while he pulled up his tighty-whities, a tire track decorating the back.

Nobody fun to talk to tonight. Avoiding Diane and the smack on the head that's inevitable if I piss her off again. I watched a talk show about former female geeks who had succeeded in their careers, lost weight, got boob jobs, straightened their hair, and so on, and hoped to rub the transformation in the faces of boys (now men) who harassed them as kids.

Of course, the asshole men refused to apologize. Not one man took responsibility for his behavior. Their common line: We Were Kids! A guy with a sensitive ponytail argued that his childhood victim still looked like a dog. And, truth be told, the girl hadn't grown into a lovely swan. She smiled grimly, absorbing his new insults—an ugly duckling wearing orange foundation and frosted, pink lipstick. Back for more abuse.

The worst part was that the women wanted the affirmation of these men. I just wanted the fucker dead.

These women appeared on national television to face the real possibility that the same bullies might say more horrible things. Like Rob may claim that I enjoyed screwing him. Maybe he tells his frat-boy friends that I asked for it rough. If Rob and I were on that show and some asshole cheered him, I'd pull out a gun. I'd press the tip into his gut and blow his stomach apart.

January 5

Well, my editor decided I'm brilliant, and I don't dare disagree with her. Dear Sue declares that I, in my silk teddy and fluttering, gold eyelashes, am the next Emily Dickinson! She's laughing here next to me, but I'm stunned by her compliment. (Though, really, I've no idea who this Dickinson person is.) OW! She hit me! Okay, I know the hermit lady. Didn't she write "A Rose By Any Other Name"? OW! I'm kidding. I hate editors looming over my shoulder. Oops, now she's leaving me. Hey! Oh, never mind, she's only making us tea.

And, meanwhile, I'll include this little ditty of a poem (at Sue's insistence) that I wrote yesterday:

BANE *by Tess*

> A woman I know
> wears a fur coat
> with a puckered pink ass on the back
> and nails that dig into her shoulders.
>
> Appearing at dinner parties,
> she drapes her monkey over the back of an armchair,
> where it lies, fuming, hissing stench
> out of its pursed rectum,
> until she can dismiss it no longer.
> Glaring, cursing, she grinds her soft teeth
> and jams her hands into the tight, heavy armholes.
>
> Slumping under its weight, barely able
> to lift a champagne glass to her lips,
> she leaves early, takes a cab home,
> sweating from the extra skin.
>
> Face first, she collapses,
> onto her bed. The hood
> flops up, its snout smacking
> her closed, wet eye.

(Heh, heh, heh)

January 6

Lucky me. I received another lecture from Diane because Swing Tony complained that I was Crude! (Remember A pussy is a pussy is a pussy?)

There's no reason to act like a slut, Diane said.

Huh? What? We're supposed to be the potty-mouth girls that men masturbate over. So I didn't guess one asshole's preference. Excuse me! I was improvising!

Screw her; I'm in a good mood.

I watched *Bull Durham* with Erin. Susan Sarandon is the sexiest woman alive. I want her breasts. I also want Erin's breasts. Actually, any big, round, perfect breasts will do. Anyone? Free breasts?

Erin and I went to breakfast together after work. We took a taxi to an all-night diner in the East Village and ate French toast. Perfect spot to take Sam.

Turns out that Erin and a friend rode a Greyhound to escape a small town in Louisiana—right out of a movie.

She picked prostitution because she needed money pronto and thought strip clubs wouldn't want luscious bodies like hers, which is not true in the average-Joe clubs. Managers know that guys possess a variety of fetishes. Erin also worried that her dark personality might intimidate guys.

Over pancakes, I explained how stripping doesn't require an outgoing personality, and how I'm actually quiet with most strangers. You need a subtle aggressiveness, an ability to ask men who rejected you an hour before if they want a lap dance now. Convince guys that the sight of you will blow their minds. Even though the same body pranced naked on stage two minutes ago, they have no idea what is in store! (Rubbing your ass on their lap is often The Surprise, if you're willing. Some girls' fingers enhance the dance. And others play it straight. I've done them all.) So you can either act like a snaky, mysterious stripper (me) or a good-time gal.

I told Erin, Good-time gals usually make more money.

I shared the story of Candy, the most popular stripper at Baby Dolls, who defined the good-time-gal image. She only worked for a few more weeks after I started, but she impressed me as an incredible dancer. Sexy and controlled, with this pinup body and long, blonde hair. She'd wear cheerleader outfits, lots of crop tops and short shorts, so a slice of her beautiful butt peeked out. Perfection in all the *Playboy*, traditional-male-fantasy ways.

Anyway, I didn't know her that well, but rumors flew that she planned to leave town to join her lesbian lover in California. And at 4:00 a.m., on her last night at Baby Dolls, she swaggered onto the stage in her five-inch heels and started dancing slow and sexy, which is not the typical three-song progression (usually, you start fast and gradually ease into bedroom mode). She began on her knees, arched her back like a cat, and skimmed her nipples on the floor, pulling up her skirt and slapping her ass hard as she gazed at the men lining the stage.

The next song had a moderate beat. She plucked loose the bows that kept her dress laced over her breasts.

I drank a rum-and-Coke that this jock paid good money for, except—as was protocol—the rum was left out of the mix, leaving me sharp enough to keep up the hustle.

Under the pink dress, Candy wore a bra and this crazy g-string, the kind that men wear on their wedding night, with a mini-tux to cover their cock. Big and limp over her crotch, she acted as if nothing was out of the ordinary, just kept dancing, and the men didn't seem to notice. Her bra dropped, and the audience was entranced. Then she unbuckled her white high heels, slipped them off, and skipped around the stage, her heavy breasts bouncing, thudding down on her rib cage.

When the last song started—rough, screaming heavy metal—she plastered on this look of shock, covering her mouth. Then, stomping one bare foot to the beat, she began punching her fist out to the side like a headbanger, closing her eyes and nodding her head in rhythm. After ten beats, she threw back and ground the saggy, tuxedo g-string against her pussy with one hand. Like a lion, she leapt and grabbed a hold of the wheel on top of the dance pole and spun herself around, screaming, I'LL BE SEEING YOU BUNCH OF PRICKS!

She jumped down, swung her head in a circle—and yanked her blonde mane OFF! All the men gasped.

Head as bald as a basted turkey.

Her tongue flopped from side to side, like the singer from Kiss, and all the strippers laughed. I was clapping. Others hooted and danced. And all the while, she banged her head, kicking the pole, yanking her body around, screaming profanities.

After that, I wanted a family in that world. So I quit Abe's Agency, which booked me at numerous clubs, and worked exclusively at Baby Dolls. Of course, I never fit into the stripper subculture, with all its stories and secrets (I was too analytical, or too aware of what I was doing, or maybe I wasn't really able to let go), but I fell in love for a while, until the men outweighed the girls and the stress outweighed the liberation.

Oh, it's a fun story to write though.

January 7

I'm wide awake, crying. Sue is on a date with a lawyer from her new temp office, so I can't talk to anyone.

Gary came in and picked Erin. Can you believe that shit? Picked her to upset me. My hands actually shook when he led her out of the Living Room.

She gave me an apologetic grimace, which I ignored. They gallivanted off to Room 3 and fucked for an hour while I smoked in the Lounge.

Then he requested me! Rich guys do this—stay in one room asking for more girls. Anyway, I refused until Diane told me that he didn't want sex. He only wanted to talk. On the intercom, she said, Tess, you can't pass this up. Easy money! You need to boost your clientele, considering your shaky reputation recently.

So, under threat, I headed upstairs. And in the southwestern room, Gary hid under the ugly orange-and-brown blanket. He wanted to stay for half an hour (cheap prick) and handed me the money without looking me in the face. I left to hide the money, as usual, but I didn't go back for fifteen minutes. Anxious, but screw him.

I smoked in the Lounge, brushed off Erin's apologies, chatted with Janice about the latest talk show where transsexuals revealed themselves to their lovers. This burly dude punched his doe-eyed lover, busting his mouth so blood slid out of the corners. Janice said that she'd do the same thing. Anyway, listening to a self-righteous hooker didn't help my mood.

After I finished my second cigarette, I walked back upstairs, threw wet laundry into the dryer, and snapped on a pair of latex gloves to put the dirty sheets into the washer. Not knowing what more to do, I meandered toward his door.

As I walked in, Gary shot me a sulky look. I strode over to the dimmer switch, which was way down, and cranked up the light until every corner of the room shone. I said, You wanted to talk?

He squinted and cringed against the pillows. The bronze moon above the bed blazed to life. In the corner stood a sombrero that I'd never noticed before, red sequins sparkling around its edges.

You used me, Gary said. (His exact words.)

I wanted to leave immediately but decided to hear his newest lies. This should be rich, I said. I walked over to the sombrero, picked it up, and made a show of examining the gold stitching.

He slowly climbed out of bed. An empty penis swung between his legs. He pulled one of the steamed towels out of the heater, wiping himself.

After our last talk, he said, I realized that you dated me as a tease, to lure me back here to spend money.

Please! You would've spent plenty of money on me even if I hadn't gone out with you.

He argued, I might've gotten bored and seen other girls.

I doubt it, I said, considering that you were In Love with me. Anyway, I never even thought about other girls making money off of you.

And I thought about Erin and how his penis was wet before it touched the steamed towel. My stomach grew tight and hot. I took a breath and held my stance, the carpet tangling around my heels.

Like you're that naïve, he said, scoffing, suddenly looking bitter and ugly.

I charged at him. How dare this weak, pathetic man act as if I'm the idiot, I thought. I stopped a foot from him, not brave enough to really get in his face. Listen, motherfucker, I said, you don't know shit about me.

He grabbed his penis and said, I know you can't handle this!

I would have laughed, but I was too confounded by having once felt connected to this guy. I stared through a telescope at some strange naked man. Who are you? I asked. Do I know you? What do you want?

He let his dick fall between his legs again.

I saw by the clock on the nightstand that I had ten minutes left.

Suddenly his arms wrapped around my waist, and he pushed his face into my neck. I tried to step away, but his arm tightened enough to make my heart bang up into my throat. I'm sorry, he muttered a few times. Told me he went crazy-jealous at the idea of other customers, that I refused to see him. Like he wasn't good enough.

A sharp pain shot through my temple, and I smelled sex coming from his face—Erin. The bright lights of the room warmed my chest, choking my throat as I realized that I didn't even know this man biting my earlobe. But he knew where I lived.

I walked over to the bed, swallowing, listening to the hum of the heating vent. The soft comforter caved under my hands as I sat down.

I said, I'm too messed up for a relationship.

He rubbed my breasts, which were sore from the last guy, and pulled at my tight, red dress.

I put out a hand, dropped to my knees, and wondered if he forgot the number of my building or at least my apartment—there's a five on the door, but it looks like a three from far away, so maybe he'll be confused by the memory.

I removed a mint condom from my purse, swallowing hard again, saliva stringing from the roof of my mouth to my tongue.

He leaned over, pushed my underwear aside, and jammed his fingers inside, hurting.

Afterward, Gary smiled when I whispered, I won't see you anymore. He said he'd still hope for a call and whistled on his way out.

Ever since, I've been seeing Rob spinning his keys around his pointer finger, talking to Misty. I stood by the kegs, watching them talk. He hugged her briefly. Across the field, sparks shot up from the campfire. No one stood to leave. There were only rows of cars and trucks parked like frontier wagons, and poor guitar playing echoing off the barn wall. So I jogged over to Misty.

Hey! she said and rubbed my back, smelling of patchouli and cigarettes. What's up?

Long time no see, Rob said and smiled at me.

Yeah, I said. I shifted on my feet so that I faced her. Hey, Mist, are you going home soon?

Well, I haven't gotten a chance to talk to you-know-who. (A crush forgotten the next week.)

I'm leaving, Rob said. If you want a ride.

Misty nodded at me, raising an eyebrow.

I looked down at the damp grass. I never had been comfortable around him.

Anyway, Rob said, the road is calling me. See ya, Misty. You're welcome to come, Tess. He strolled off toward his truck.

Misty hugged me. I'll see you tomorrow. He's fine. Ate 'shrooms earlier, but he's coming down. He's the only one leaving for at least an hour.

I sighed and kissed her on the cheek. Clambering into Rob's truck, I thanked him. He didn't respond. Turned his thin, veined neck in a hard circle and gripped my headrest as he backed down the dirt road.

Feeling for an update on his sobriety status, I teasingly asked him if he'd had a nice mushroom trip.

He smiled and said, I'm going to keep tripping till school starts again. Tripping keeps reality at bay, he said, talking fast and clipped. I noticed that his nose had a pockmark on the tip.

As we passed the Harrisons', I calculated that we'd gone two miles. Only six miles left with welcome heat warming my toes.

His gaze turned my way a few times.

He eased the truck over to the side of the road and flipped open the glove compartment. He pulled out a pill bottle, orange with no label, and offered me one.

Another time, I said. I gotta pack.

No cops come this way, he said. He threw back one.

Then he pressed the gas pedal, making the engine rev as he smiled at me. He popped the truck into drive and pulled back onto the road. Trees slid by. I remember tree branches running over the bright stars. Thinking, He's harmless.

You've done drugs, haven't you?

I smiled politely at him. I've indulged in a joint or two.

He pounded the wheel with his fist, surprising me with his aggression. Don't tell me that Little Miss Attitude has never tried speed!

Irritation rose. No thank you, I said.

He slid to the side of the road again.

Rob, I said, I need to go home, not get high right before I see my parents. I rolled down the window and lit a cigarette, refusing to explain more.

He tossed the bottle onto the floor by my feet, saying, Fine.

Headlights moved toward us, and I actually wondered if I should hop out and ask for a ride back to the party, not wanting to deal with a drugged-out driver.

I won't write about the rest of the night.

I gotta learn. Tonight I was blindsided by Gary's attack. He cracked me without even trying. I was too afraid to breathe, let alone ask him to respect me. I'm pathetic. Pacifying him with a blowjob.

> There was a young woman from Lenore
> Whose mouth was as wide as a door.
> While attempting to grin,
> She slipped and fell in,
> And lay inside out on the floor.

January 8

This evening, in the kitchen window that's painted shut, a butterfly fluttered between my screen and pane. She circled, crawled, and dragged her wings until they hung in tatters, the glitter gone, ashes at her feet. And she stared at me, wondering how, in my right mind, I kept working. I didn't have an answer for her, so I trudged out into the snow.

I only saw Hairy Frank, his back like a gorilla, because oral sex and a back rub satisfy him. He doesn't demand intercourse, just loves it when you touch his back.

Otherwise, I refused to participate in the lineup. I stayed in the Lounge listing excuses for not greeting guys.

Eventually, Erin cornered me, asking, What the hell's wrong?

I pointed down and whispered, No in-and-out for me tonight. I'm sore. Luckily Diane skipped work, so no one raised an eyebrow.

I mostly slept in the Lounge—pretended to feel nauseous at one point, faked a long headache, passed on all of my regulars. I turned down a session with a businessman I'd seen before, claiming that he smacked my ass too hard, which is true. I don't care how little money I make.

Sue suggested the excuses—wonderful, wonderful friend. When I told her about Gary, she wanted me to quit. But I want to hide out in the barracks, away from the apartment.

I'm considering stripping again, running away from a job that may leave me a corpse who played her own rapist. Asked how I contracted AIDS, I'd say that I got raped—by myself and this fat forty-year-old fuck who helped out.

So, while I ran my fingers over Frank, my red nails sliding through the grass on his back, I carefully watched his hands lying still on the pillows. I checked the screwdriver sticking out the top of my purse, easy to grab if I hung over the side of the bed. I hummed to keep calm, told him to keep his eyes closed and concentrate on my touch, and raised the volume of the soothing jazz music. And I wore my red, lacy underwear at all times.

Oh, fuck it. I'm quitting. I've decided. I'll nail this underwear onto my hips, to be removed in five or ten years when the smell is ungodly and I'm sure that no one will ever pull down my underpants again without asking or loving.

I'll give blowjobs for the two more weeks that I'm scheduled to work. Diane never said anything about proper notice, so when it's time to sign up for more nights, I'll tell her I need a couple weeks off and never return. She won't come after me. Girls apply for my job constantly.

Stripping, I'm back. Even lonely and lost in the glitter, safety existed inside strip clubs with the other girls watching and cheering.

So, it's final (unless Diane threatens to kill me): not another dick presses toward my heart.

I'm just like the girls on talk shows. The accused slut stands— fourteen, sixteen years old, sticking out her chin, giving the finger, beaten down by an audience roaring with self-righteous indignation because this girl won't cower in front of them. But in the end, the audience wins, and that's the truth. No matter how many times she shakes her head, calls them *whores* back, or tells the Fat Cows in the audience to sit down, her pain makes them win.

I'm the same with men, as dumb a slut as the rest. With me, they win. Not with every hooker, but with me. I buckle from the pain.

But hope is here. They won for a while, but watch me now.

January 9

I'm so eager to quit, I'm practically falling off my chair. Tonight I serviced tons of guys—well, three, but that's a lot since the holidays.

My jaw aches and my tongue tingles. Goofy images roll through my mind—sitting on the end of a bed singing praises to The Cock, rocking my head from side to side with minty dicks swirling saliva into mouthwash, rolling balls like I'm playing marbles. Funny to be so focused.

With tonight's loot added in, I've managed to save a fair chunk of cash, so I don't need to worry if it takes a few weeks to settle into stripping. And since my oral enthusiasm tickles customers, nobody will complain to Diane.

Erin and Sarah are disgusted by my success. At first, Erin didn't believe that I managed to avoid intercourse.

I leaned back and told her to crawl on her knees and smell it for herself.

She laughed so hard that she smeared the lipstick she was applying. Then she turned all serious, sipping bourbon disguised in a twenty-ounce pop bottle, and said, You're too cocky for your own good.

Sarah, gaunt and pale these days, practically took notes on what I'd told guys. She's not cut out for this work. She's too sweet and dating a guy she digs. Both said that I'll only escape scrutiny because my strike is temporary, which is true. Also, I couldn't put on such a show if I didn't see an end in sight.

Diane did stare at me as I dressed to leave. She said, Expensive panties you're wearing tonight, Estelle. Her eyes skimmed over the ruffled waistline of my underwear.

But I bet she didn't hear much—just that I'm focusing on oral sex. Nothing I can do but lie low anyway. Stick to the plan.

Okay, enough! Gods of humor, help this humorless wench!

> There once was a man from Nantucket,
> Whose dick was so long he could suck it.
> He said with a grin, while wiping his chin,
> If my ear was a cunt, I would fuck it.

January 10

Wow. I ran into my apartment and took the longest pee ever! I think I broke the world record. After the initial rush, it trickled out for another forty seconds, I swear. I only peed once at work. Hmmm. Fascinating.

Worked a double with Erin. She convinced her regular, Marcus, to order me too, because he fools around a few times before he's willing to have intercourse with a girl. A nice guy. Goofy with his gaspy laugh, but nice. We amused him. She slapped my ass, so I smacked back. We traded off straddling each other's backs, like in a rodeo, waving our lassoes. Then Erin massaged his rear while I went down on him. He loved it. I found myself enjoying the insanity.

January 11

For the first two hours of work I sat in the Lounge, faking a headache until Auto Mike came in, and I let him pick me, he's so laid-back.

Soon after, Dave the Bear arrived, a regular of mine who loves intercourse, so I didn't go into the Living Room. Five minutes later, I heard a commotion, and Diane appeared in the doorway.

Clear Out! She nodded to Erin and Sarah.

On the couch, I hunched over the pages of *Cosmo*.

Shutting the door, she lumbered across to me, breathing onto the top of my head. So, honey—using her sexy phone voice—I hear you conjured up a headache.

Knowing I was screwed, I stared at the pink, blotchy skin rolling over the edges of her tennis shoes. I held my throat, feigning sickness. Yeah, I said, it's pretty bad. I'll schedule an extra day to make up the hours. I promise. I should probably just nap.

I lowered myself onto my side, discarded newspaper crackling under my ear. I focused my eyes on the NASCAR race whirling inside the TV.

She leaned toward my face.

I threw up my hands, and my eyes slammed shut. I waited for the punch, trying to stuff my face between my knees. Car engines roared.

Tess, she asked, are you scared of the Big Bad Wolf? Worried I might hire someone to break your neck? Bash your skull in? You shouldn't bite off more than you can chew, but you can ponder that on your own time. For now, you will fuck, lick, suck, and be licked by any client who deigns to enter this house.

Listen, I said. I'm quitting. All right. I'm quitting. Please. Please. Please.

Oh, shut up and stop begging. You're scheduled for two more nights, and then we'll be done. Got it? Don't you try to weasel out of those days either, or your fears might come true.

With one palm, Diane pushed the side of my head into the cushions and let it spring back up, slapping onto the newspaper.

She left. And I heard the girls saying, How are you? Did you know it was coming? You should have run.

I remembered Rob holding me up, punching the back of my head a few times to chill me out, my knees swinging slightly above ground. My chin shot forward, my stomach and crotch following like a waterbed wave. You better—fucking—cooperate, he said, punctuating each word with a punch.

For the event, he picked a prime spot about a mile from my house, suddenly turning the truck down a hollow where a bunch of hippies used to live. No one could hear shit from back there.

I yelled at him for fooling around, as I watched the headlights bang into potholes full of grass.

Half a mile in, his hand snapped out and fisted the back of my hair, yanking me around so I faced away from him. My body and hands flailed, hitting back at the wheel and grazing his thighs.

Hold still, he roared as I threw my body forward, my scalp pulling tight, strands of hair ripping out above my ear, the window visor knocked off by my elbows. The brakes slammed, and we rocked to a stop. I should've screamed, but I only grunted, squirming, trying to knock myself out of his grasp. The fight-or-flight instinct—all physical motion and quiet concentration on releasing myself. I gained enough leverage with my feet against the door to turn and drag my nails down the arm attached to my skull. His skin scraped off as I dug for blood.

He let go with a push.

Free, I fell toward the door.

He jumped on me, his ribs sticking into my back as he licked my ear. I think he said, Let's fuck. I barely heard, my head beating with panic.

I jerked my head forward and swung it back into his face, hitting bone. I jerked the handle and threw open my door. Run! Go, Go, Go! I yelled in my head.

But he caught me. Raped me. Simple.

Fucking Diane.

January 12

Last night I climbed into bed with Sue, and we snuggled, her arms cool like my mother's. She asked me what I write about these days.

I said, I'm nostalgic for stripping.

Promise me, she said, that you'll check out a club before you choose that option.

So this evening I worked a few hours at Sugar Palace.

In clubs, the floodlights wash out all the details, smoothing a line of ivory foundation under the chin. Girls hide beneath eye shadow and music. We are pieces of flesh with bits of red ribbon for gentlemen callers.

The Sugar Palace was no different. The mirrors there distracted me, and the smoke disguised odors, smeared faces. I walked offstage, down the curving carpet, into the arms of a guy who might've smirked or smiled for all I could tell.

I sought refuge in the dressing room—old habits dying hard. In front of the mirror, I slumped close to my reflection over compacts and tote bags. My eyes were bloodshot. Mascara clumped my lashes together Loneliness drained the stars from my skylights. I missed Erin; Sue, too.

The few hours felt like a strip club at closing time, when the stale, acidic smell has soaked into the spongy skin of the guys and dolls, and the lights snap to bright, and you know you're a different creature—not pretty, funny, or sexy. Too skinny, with half-hidden pimples, a sore knee, and scuffed five-inch heels with skid pads stuck to the soles.

A twenty-year-old girl wearing a clingy, white, velvet "gown" with a neckline plunging to her bellybutton, a dress not even Dolly Parton could get away with. Tonight, I didn't buy any of it.

What am I to do? Reevaluate West Virginia—home?

A funny man, a club customer who didn't know my day job, told me a limerick:

> There once was a man named Dave,
> Who kept a dead whore in a cave.
> She had only one tit and smelled worse than shit,
> But think of the money Dave saved . . .

January 13

Sweet, steady Whistling John ate me out and then rubbed my clit. I told my old buddy, No need. I said, I'm already wet and excited. (I sound like a bad *Penthouse* letter when I try to rush guys.)

He ignored me. He blew in my ear, licked my earlobe. And suddenly, he ground in the tip of his finger. I jolted, and his nail jammed in. The motherfucker cut me.

I ran to the bathroom, wondering (still wondering) if Diane set him up. But I'm scared of another complaint reaching her, so I pressed a wad of toilet paper on the bloody spot and scurried back to the bedroom. Don't worry, I said, you just hit a sore area; better let it have a rest. I kneeled down, my heart pounding. My hands shook as I unrolled the condom.

Man, I yelled into his crotch, you are one big, furry monkey.

His confusion obvious, I held onto my stomach as I laughed, until his hands cupped the back of my head and directed my mouth.

The slice opens right above my clit. The skin is slightly opened, pink, an inch long.

Work has changed my pussy. Looking at the flesh under a lamp, the lips have grown darker, browner rather than berry-colored. Pulling them apart, I feel harder bumps under the surface. The edges look more pronounced, calloused almost. Covered by my pubic hair, the entire area is brown and rough.

Luckily, I have a few days off before my last night of work, so I can try out a liquid sealant that Erin suggested. Yes, I need glue to hold my pussy together.

January 16

Yesterday Gary telephoned, whispering over and over, Meet me, please? until I hung up.

He called back twice, and I yelled at him to shut up, waited for a second, and then listened to him repeat his fucking question. He's probably crouching behind our apartment door, a gun in his hand. Following me around town. Sue says that he isn't officially stalking until a week of phone calls.

I'd buy a gun from a pawn shop, but I imagine he'd just yank it out of my hands and use the bullets on me.

Better alive and raped than dead and raped.

I'm running off to West Virginia again. I packed for hours today, labeling boxes and wrapping up half of my CDs. Hauling precious items back home to where it's safe—pictures, china animals, my marijuana headpiece, my signed Jesco White picture.

I'm presently lying on our couch in my pj's with my comforter over me. Sue's across the room watching a stupid sitcom, eating a huge piece of my chocolate cake, laughing her head off because she's scared and depressed that she can't find anyone to love. She's pretending not to notice the suitcases on my bed. My back hurts. My head aches. I panicked earlier—shocker. The attack lasted two hours. I indulged in a pity party, feeding the fear with more images.

First image: When Rob punched, white light flashing. Second image: Diane, the forceful pressure of her hand, my head swelling off the cool newspapers. Third image: Whistling John's teeth on my earlobe, my slit vagina.

Taking a shower, I collapsed on the rusted floor, sucking on the M&M's Sue bought me, shaking and crying. Red, brown, green, and yellow puddles stained my palms. Trails of water slid down the gray shower walls.

One more night of work.

January 17

Gary telephoned for the second day, calling me a slut. I left the apartment and wandered Chinatown, storming into Washington Park to sullenly watch mah-jongg players click and clack in the freezing cold.

I rode the subway uptown around dinnertime.

When I first visited NYC, I fell in love with Times Square. The lights, the bustle, the combination of class and trash in the people and the theaters. I loved it. I wanted to feel as alive as those streets.

Today, snow flurries dusted my hair as I tried on sunglasses at the year-round sale rack. I bought a slice of pizza, watched flashing advertisements for the Gap. Wonderful as always, but I'm finished.

Squatting on a traffic island in the middle of New York, I decided. We're through. My exhilaration has dissipated.

Home seems a fine retreat, at least until Rob visits. Buying a car is my first priority, for rides out of town at a moment's notice, fast getaways.

Back at the apartment, I packed Pandy's toys and most of my clothes and shoes. Hard to imagine cramming all of this stuff into the tiny bedroom at home. It's too late to call, so tomorrow I'll tell Ma to remove her knickknacks and find me some storage. My futon alone will swallow my floor space.

I signed a lease, but I hope Sue realizes that I need to leave, sees that I hobble up stairs because my knees hurt from kneeling and wearing high heels, is moved by the fact that I still panic even though I supposedly know how to control the attacks. Pamphlets can only get you so far.

I wish Rob was lying in grass next to the truck and I could kick the shit out of him, crush huge dents in the side of his skull, and cause brain damage so he'd literally never think about raping again. I'd kick my sharp toenails so far up his asshole, I'd tear a hole in his intestines, and he'd walk around carrying a sack in his pocket where his shit drained because his bowels didn't work. A shit bag would slow him down.

I fought him, you know, until he pulled out a knife, dug the tip into my rib cage, and said that he'd slip it right through, to the Heart Of The Matter, if I continued fucking around.

Oh, hell. Back to the country. I'll miss the beat of New York, but I can't keep the pace. I am not as tough as I'd hoped.

January 18

Ma's so excited, she didn't mention Sam once. She asked me if I wanted her to paint my room a new color. Dad jumped on the other line and asked if I planned to go back to school. I said I didn't know yet.

Gotta finish that degree some lifetime, he said. Remember, Davis and Elkins has a good reputation.

Stop harassing her, Ma said.

Dad said he wants to retrieve me on January 22. (The sooner, the better, I think.) He also whispered that Ma's been going to Al-Anon every week and coping with Sam a lot better.

Ma huffed that he didn't need to whisper, as if she's recovering from a nervous breakdown or something.

He ignored her and continued the whispered teasing. She wants to go on dates with me, he said, like we're teenagers.

Says the man who's whispering on the phone like a *true* teenager, Ma retorted.

Funny folks.

I broke the news to Sue while we were discussing her potential preppy boyfriend over dinner at Excellent Malaysian. I suggested that he move in and replace me.

Silent, she chewed her broccoli stems like they were pieces of steak, and I couldn't break her out of that space.

I'm exhausted, I said. I need to go home.

She shot back, You signed a lease. And how about showing me a little consideration?

I told her that I'd pay February's rent and offered to help find a new roommate.

She let her hair slip forward, so that it hid her face, and muttered about loyalty.

Humiliated by her ability to distance herself from me—like I'm pleading with a stranger—I cried.

She cooled down, saying she was sorry. She moaned that she hates change. We're only beginning to grow tight, she said. It's not right to dump a friend like they're just a boy.

Her mouth stayed stiff, angry in the corners. She excused herself to the bathroom.

I waited, smoking. I kept thinking, She's my only real friend.

When she sat back down, I said, I'll put an ad in the paper for a roommate.

She still looked upset.

Oh, sweetie, I said, let me go, let me leave. I can't write about all the guys I screw anymore. I can't write about my pathetic attempts at love. I can't write about dicks, fear, semen, insecurity, depression, body odor, or any more of this life, because it doesn't make sense and it's not worth the damage. I'm on the edge of cracking, and my pussy is turning into a raisin.

Back at the apartment, she's calmer now, calling me a butterfly—too beautiful to keep even if you do catch one.

Finding a true friend makes leaving harder.

January 19

Ma called and described her recent work on a large canvas. The trees (inspired by our ears) frame the body of the painting. She's also working on a pencil drawing of our fireplace with me and Sam hiding in the ash.

I described talk shows. I said that men need to be jailed for not paying child support, or that the government should sell their houses out from under them. And all the shows should hire smart shrinks, like they did in the past. If people share their problems and television executives profit from them, at least offer professional help! Hosts don't bother anymore.

Ma didn't understand my vehemence, but she made sounds of agreement—Mmm-hmm, mmm-hmm.

And hearing her empathy made me want to confess about the rape—badly. It hung on my tonsils, and if somebody had hit me between the shoulder blades, it would've flown out.

January 20

I went out with a bang. Gary called to schedule a session with me, but Diane lectured him about needing to take some space, see another girl for a while. He's probably harmless, but I'm too paranoid to be able to clearly assess the situation. Let Diane handle him.

I only saw Blue Ben, who the girls secretly call Ben Gay because he's in the closet. He's a handsome man with a wrestler's body. He wanted me to lie on my back in the Linda Lovelace position so that my head hung back off the bed, my body limp, while he pushed his half-mast penis down my throat. My neck kept cramping afterward, but at least he didn't want intercourse.

Erin had warned me that he liked vibrators in his rear, and eventually this gorgeous guy blushed and asked for his PB & J, apologizing for grossing me out.

Whatever floats your boat, I said and dug into the closet to find the bag of vibrators that I had never used before. I'm not grossed out, I continued, meaning it, but still, I shoved my fingers into latex gloves as a safety precaution. I'll be gentle, I reassured him. Don't worry.

He lay face down on the bed. Would you speak with a deep voice, please? he asked.

I quietly turned back the comforter and inserted the dildo, gently.

He scooted away, tense and shaking. On the far side of the bed, he gasped a few breaths and cried for a second, and I thought we were through.

Try again, he said into the pillow. Please, smaller.

I had used the smallest. Feeling sad for him, I lubricated my middle finger, and he got off.

Afterward, his hands covered his whole face. His gold watch dangled loosely on his wrist, shining in the dim light as he cried. Poor guy.

In the armchair, I slipped a cigarette out of my pack and casually said that he shouldn't feel ashamed, that all sorts of sexual preferences exist, and his was natural, fine.

The only disgusting part, which I didn't say, was ME. Sticking my finger in the wrinkled folds of some stranger's asshole, hurting this mixed-up guy, helping him hurt himself. I'm ashamed.

But I am finished. Diane bought me a cake covered with big cherries and red letters that spell out Don't Forget Who Broke You In! They laughed and joked. Like I'm going to be a hugely famous whore one day and, on my deathbed, whisper out a word of thanks to Diane's catering girls.

After a couple forkfuls of cake, I ran to the bathroom, blood rushing to my face, and vomited.

See, once I got Rob's car door open, I tripped in the ditch outside. He landed on me again. My knees ground over rocks as I fell onto my stomach.

I bucked, pushing with my arms. Get off, I grunted.

He whispered, Don't be so noisy.

I remember his damp, sweet deodorant in my face, him grabbing my armpit and flipping me over, the back of my head thudding against the packed dirt.

He pressed the end of a Swiss Army knife into my chest. If you don't shut up, he announced loudly, yet calmly, we'll get to the Heart Of The Matter. Light from the truck made his stubble look blue; his lips looked puffy in the corners. Red-rimmed eyes.

I expected even the branches to straighten in shock.

No, I said softly. Rob, don't do this. You don't know what this will do to me. (I knew, right then, a dread for my reaction.) Let me go. Please, please. I slid my hands out, searching for a rock to slam him in the head with, like in the movies.

He pressed the blade through the flannel shirt I stole from Sam until the knifepoint broke layers of my skin. Blood wet the cotton.

And suddenly, another me floated by the tree line and watched from out in the woods as some skinny guy with hiking boots and a bomber jacket pulled down his pants. Pasty legs.

On an overgrown dirt road, he lifted a girl up by her hair, her trench coat slipping off onto the ground, the moonlight around them. He punched her head, once directly on top, as if to pound her down into the ground.

Don't kill me: the words rose out of me. My body swung with each punch, my arms limp at my side. When he finished, I collapsed.

Responding to orders, I stayed on my knees, looking at his thick pubic hair. And, leaning forward, my face white and dry, hands out to the side, I touched his dick with my closed lips and my head fell back.

The semen strung from my mouth to his penis, snapping against my chin, hanging there.

Rob grabbed either side of my head with the knife still in his hand, the handle hard against my temple. He slammed my face against his penis; its wet tip smeared my eyelid.

He dropped to his knees, setting aside the knife, and grabbed my top and bottom teeth with both hands. He pulled, jacking open my mouth as wide as it would go, and I moaned, my jaw stretched so, so tight, my tongue flapping helplessly, the corners of my mouth splitting as I began to cry. I breathed in and choked on my tears, coughing.

And again, he yanked me down on his penis. This time I remembered to open my mouth. I reared back gagging.

I'll kill you if you puke!

And again, he jerked my head up and down, my mouth open, stiff, in and out of my mouth, the smell of rotten milk easing up my nasal passages as he jerked my ears, again, again, nails digging in behind them.

And I let him, no resistance. I didn't care about rape anymore. Don't kill me, I thought. I just wanted to live.

I watched the knife as I bent over it again and again, looking for a chance.

But his climax beat my reflexes. Swallow! he yelled in my face.

But my throat locked. I tried. I just wanted to live.

I swallowed. My stomach, as if grabbed in a fist, revolted and sent Thanksgiving dinner and Rob up and out of my torn throat. I turned to the side to keep the puke off of him as he picked up the knife.

I lay panting. I don't know how long.

He stood, looking around. Eventually he lay on top of me.

A few sticks rested nearby—one had a green twig growing out of its side, and another lay dead, straight and thick, and I considered gouging him, until a searing pain punctured the thought. And the breeze grew hot and dug into my skin like a sunburn.

I don't remember any more. The next thing I knew, I was in his truck in front of my house, my hair was loose, and the coat that had passively watched from the ground was on me and buttoned to the top, as if by a parent.

I was thinking, Sam will kill him for me. I gotta talk to Sam. Get a gun, hold a gun in my hand, heavy—one that would fit in a glove compartment, and I could find him.

Rob licked his thumb and rubbed a spot on the side of my neck.

I slid out of the truck, my head like a thirty-pound bucket of water balancing on my neck. Shoot me in the back, I thought. Go ahead. Do it or you'll die.

He said, See ya later, Tess. Maybe I'll drop by Misty's tonight and ask her if you called. If you tattle, I might have to teach her a lesson, too. And I stopped and looked at the light in the living room window, and I walked toward it. The breeze hurt.

I figured that he had found a gun, made one. I imagined him taking aim to blast a hole in my neck so I couldn't say his name or describe his crime.

January 21

As I finished packing today, I sang that song from *My Fair Lady* (well, I sang what I could remember of it):

Just you wait, Henry Higgins, just you wait! You'll cry, but your cries will be too late. As they raise the guns higher, I'll shout READY, AIM, FIRE! Yo ho ho, Henry Higgins. Down you'll go, Henry Higgins. Just! You! Wait!

I imagine bitch-slapping slow store clerks, street vendors yelling in my ears, old men playing mah-jongg. Why don't they go home and rub their wives' feet?

Therapy is a must. I need to learn contentment, find joy again. I don't want to die a tragic cliché of the screwed-up girl. I don't want to become Mae West, who ended her life as a caricature of the witty hooker she'd played for years—stage makeup rerouting plain features, corsets defining a waist. They say the girl before Mae West was wiped out.

Destroying yourself can take on many forms. And the danger exists that, unless my life changes, I will erect my own prison of fear and lose myself in those walls, with anxiety dominating my every action. As it is, I raped myself more than Rob ever did. I pulled penises inside my cramped vagina . . . to test my limits?

I guess I manage terror too well.

January 22: Arrival

Dad is asleep on the floor, sprawled out on a torn sleeping bag that he brought. My faux-fur coat serves as a blanket for Sam snoring on my couch.

Their only other protection against Sue's fifty-degree sleeping temperature is long underwear, and who wears long underwear anymore? Lumpy things.

I'm lying in bed, petting Pandy. She's distressed by the chaos in the apartment. My closet is her temporary hiding place.

Seeing my men in this world is odd. They're so laid-back, taking their time. They ask Sue questions about her family rather than analyzing pop culture. They find the grocery store and make sandwiches. They remark on the architecture.

Yesterday Dad's truck rumbled to a stop in front of my apartment building. He began honking while Sam yelled my name.

I woke up, confused to hear their voices, then excited to leave my life—then scared to find myself repulsed by their strong body odors as they stomped into my small apartment. My heart picked up as they squeezed me with bear hugs.

Sam taunted, You look like a scarecrow, city girl.

I pushed his shoulder, but he didn't budge.

See, he said, I'm surprised the wind doesn't piss you off, the way it pushes you around.

Yeah, well, your face is so puffy, I'm surprised Trashy Terri settled for you.

He gasped dramatically and laughed, his new beard softening the creases of his cheeks, the bulge of his jaw.

Of course, after an hour of packing the truck, his hands began to shake so hard he grew embarrassed and excused himself to the nearest bar. Dad tried to stop him, but he skittered down the street.

Dad leaned on the truck and rubbed the sides of his nose. The big geek wore overalls to New York for some god-forsaken reason—like they're necessary. He never wears them at home.

When Dad started talking about college, I asked him to stop. First let me recover, I said.

He reached over and rubbed the back of my neck. Sorry, he said. I just don't want you to get offtrack like you-know-who.

As his rough fingers touched me, I flashed to Rob's punches, to the guys at the House. But I waited to shudder until Dad walked back into the apartment. I thought, Imagine yourself underwater, cool.

January 23: Home

I'm laughing because Ma rehung every rock-and-roll poster I ever owned as a teenager on my bedroom walls. And in the middle of all the slashing makeup and wagging tongues hangs the kitten poster that made me panic so long ago. Those scary kittens.

Drove in an hour ago. The house smells of firewood and massage oil.

Ma greeted us with milk and cookies in the kitchen. Sam and I indulged, but Dad ran to his room to shower off the foreign pollutants.

Then Sam ran away. A friend picked him up during my brief retreat to the bathroom. But the gravel crunching on the driveway didn't startle me, so maybe the haunting will ease.

I've traded my stale-smelling velvet pants, sticky from sweat, for one of Ma's nightgowns. The cool cotton is a relief after the car heater blasted and pecked at my skin, burning me, for hours.

January 24

I'm sore and hot. The flu. I hate being sick, hate it. My shoulders and neck ache whenever I move. My temperature is 102.6, and I'm obsessed with checking it every ten minutes—the digital thermometer waits on my nightstand for bouts of morbid interest. I take pride in my high temperatures. Ma's covered me with quilts, but whenever she leaves, I throw them off. The bed and I both smell like urine from sweating through the night. I want ginger ale. Ma tries to wheedle me into drinking molasses like I'm five. Now she's off buying ice cream.

God, I'm so weak. This must be my body's inevitable collapse after protecting itself for so long.

Be quiet for a while, Tess. Build up strength.

Oh, I'm bawling, and Ma's gonna come home, and how can I act like her baby? Let a swell of love rock me each time I see my family, so I can remember why I don't kill myself.

Jesus, I gotta stop writing and wipe my nose.

GOD! How dare you, motherfucker! How dare you gain this much power!

I begged you.

Later: My toes feel icy and damp.

Ma caught me crying, and she rubbed my hands with hers. She massaged the pads of my fingers, and warm sparks ran up my arms. She brought me chocolate ice cream and read me *People* magazine until I fell asleep curled around her soft hip that weighed down the edge of my bed.

January 25

My temperature hovers around 102. Ma and Dad are asleep. Strange adjusting to bedtime at eleven, the house silent and toasty. A luxury.

Tomorrow I'll muster the energy to piece together my futon. Updating the look of my room is also in order since the Bangles don't reflect my current tastes. Ma wants to help, but we've always fought about decorating—she likes straight lines and I like odd angles. She even offered to paint my walls magenta, trying to tempt me with a fifteen-year-old's dream. Lordy, lordy.

I called Sue after dinner, missing her knowledge and understanding of me. She's mad at the new roommate, Brenda, who brought too much furniture, turns up the TV too loud, and calls too many friends on the phone.

I told her to expect severe withdrawal symptoms for a while.

January 26

It's snowing like hell outside, but I'm mostly healthy again. Body temperature: 99.2.

This afternoon we needed kindling for the furnace, so I trudged into the woods with our enormous, silver wheelbarrow. I wore Dad's work gloves, ten sizes too big, and stretched my chest. A tough country girl again, I sniffed out slim pieces of wood and hurled each one into the bottom of the wheelbarrow. Bangs and grunts were the only sounds for miles except for the snow. Shaken loose by wind, it burst down through the tree limbs and stumbled on top of the white, dazed heaps already on the ground.

Back and forth, I hauled load after load, bumping and swaying over the rough ground, my feet cracking the frozen leaves that littered the forest floor.

Occasionally, I hit an evergreen patch, and smooth, brown pine needles slid me across a soft universe. I skated as I walked, riding on each small needle that rolled under my shoes.

Pandy is confused by the outdoors. She laid one paw in the icy yard and leapt back, shaking her foot, ears flat.

When I carried her back inside, Ma stopped me. I rented us the movie *Beaches*, she said. Thought we could watch it together tonight.

I don't know, Ma, I said.

I made you popcorn. I even put extra salt in your bowl, she said pleadingly.

You should have asked me first, I said, suppressing a sigh.

It appears that her new attitude, care of Al-Anon, doesn't limit itself to hot dates with Dad. I could have watched the movie, but I didn't want to encourage her. Next thing you know, she'll be wanting me to get my hair done, go clothes shopping, or talk about boys. No, thank you.

I explained to her that Pandy needed my attention and retreated to my room, curling up with my friend under the blankets.

January 27

Misty called. My mom told me that you'd moved home! she said. You should've called me!

At first I was happy to hear from her, relieved that she'd initiated the contact. I took the cordless phone into my room and plopped down on my bed. It had been hard to let my first friend go.

She said, I could come home in a couple weekends and hang out with you.

I'd like that, I said, adding that being only around family is exhausting. I pulled a pillow under my head and let the winter sun coming through the window warm my face.

Ugh, she said and laughed. I could never imagine living at home again. I'd get homicidal.

Or suicidal, I added.

Hardly, she said, scoffing. I'd bump them off first, for sure.

I grinned, glad she could still be wry about some things.

Hey, she said, maybe we could hang out with Rob when I come to town. He's grown into a good guy.

I sat up in bed, putting my fingers to my lips.

She continued. No doubt he was screwed up in high school, but getting out of his house has done wonders.

Yeah, I finally said, he was a piece of work, a real fucking piece of work.

I forced myself to relax my grip in the phone, to take a breath rather than pull my knees up to my chest as protection. What can I expect, I thought, when I never told her what happened?

But we've been hanging out, she said, and he's a really funny guy, real aware of his issues now. He and I could literally spend all night talking about life, the world.

I froze at the hint of romance.

Misty steamrolled ahead. She said, I thought maybe when I come to town, we could all go out, include Rob in a joyride. He's in Elkins this week, actually, if you want to call him. You're both probably lonely. It might be good for you guys to see each other.

What? I asked with confusion, kicking my heel against my bed frame. I kicked and kicked . . . until I simply said, You know he raped me that night he drove me home.

And the relief of saying the words to her made me smile.

Silence on her end.

Then the unbelievable. A cough and then: Tess, he said . . . Rob told me that you two had sex. Listen, now. He suspects that you regretted it. You both were high, not thinking.

All I could say was, Huh?

He told me how he called you the next day for a formal date, but you cut him off and told him it didn't mean anything, to forget it ever happened. He feels bad, still.

Misty. I'm sorry, but he did rape me. He's lying. He raped me.

Okay, okay.

You don't believe me? I said, a burst of anger heating my cheeks.

Tess, he admitted that you must've resented his behavior, that he used crude language. That's pretty brave to admit, knowing I'm your best friend.

Hey, Misty, reality check! He's covering his ass. After he finished beating the shit out of me, he threatened to rape you in order to keep me quiet.

She sighed and said, Honey . . .

In the pause that followed, I could sense her justifying it in her mind, classifying me as an Angry Sex Addict who has gone off the deep end—compared to Mournful Rob.

Remember, I began my argument, that I'd only had sex with Zach.

I have never seen Rob act violent, she argued back.

Remember how after Zach, I vowed not to have sex unless I loved the guy?

Tess . . . Her voice was cold.

Misty?

You didn't keep that vow.

I didn't see the point after the rape, I snapped.

Silence.

Misty, I said, desperation rising in me, please don't do this. You're the first one I've told who matters. You can't not believe me. I didn't tell you because I was scared of your disbelief or judgment. Don't actually live up to my fears.

Silence.

I don't know what to believe, she said. You and I aren't even close anymore.

Why would I make this up?

Maybe to hold onto me, maybe to hurt Rob. I don't know.

Holy shit, I said, you think that I'd lie about something like this?

She sighed.

I let the phone roll from my hand, numb.

Wow. I guess I waited too long. Probably no one trusts me anymore. I'm just some crazy chick.

January 28

After lunch today, Ma dropped me off at the Laundromat because our washer at home is too small for the comforter that fits my futon.

While digging in my big, red purse for a dollar to put in the change machine, I heard a woman say, Now listen for the clink and then run up and grab the money that's fallen into the slot.

And sitting a few seats away was Dee Dee, a high-school buddy, and her two-year-old daughter, Rae, who didn't understand but giggled anyway.

I said, Hey there! What are you doing here? And we hugged, taking in the changes.

Crouching down, I wiggled my fingers at Rae and threatened to tickle her if she stole my money. Rae was as pretty as her mother, though Dee Dee's soft hippie beauty had evolved, with sharper cheek-bones and longer unkempt hair. Her clothes still looked like they'd come from thrift stores, but they fit her slight frame tighter.

We fell into an easy rapport. Dee Dee told me that she moved home about a year ago after failing to break into San Francisco's theater scene. While eating M&M's from the vending machine, she said, without any self-pity, that Rae's conception right after high school had made reaching goals tougher.

I admired her for trying at least.

She asked about Misty. Tension spread across the back of my neck, but I just shrugged. Then I filled her in on New York and stripping. She gaped and said that I was the last person she could imagine as a stripper. She never thought I seemed that interested in men or their opinions.

I didn't know what to say, so I said, We ought to hang out.

She said, Hell yes. Why don't you come over now? I'll give you a ride home later? I hesitated only a second before I thought, Fuck it. Why not? So I took her up on her offer.

I left a note for Ma with the front-desk clerk, shoved my plastic bag full of clean blankets into her trunk, and sang "Old MacDonald" to Rae until she fell asleep in the car.

Soon after, we pulled up to a converted old house where the two of them live in a one-bedroom apartment. Dee Dee carried a sleeping Rae—who lay limp in her arms, breathing heavily into her mother's neck—through the stained yellow kitchen and the dark living room to the baby's bright blue bedroom and the white crib.

And then we got so baked I couldn't move.

After she put Rae down, Dee Dee rolled a fat joint, set out saltines and cheddar cheese, and popped in a porno. We laughed for an hour straight. I think the title was *Fuck, Fuck, Fuck*, but I might be forgetting one other *Fuck*.

We raised our beers to Rae's three-hour naps and cooked an omelet at one point.

For dinner, once we'd shaken off the deepest hilarity, Dee Dee whipped up a big batch of Ramen noodles, and we applauded Rae as she stuffed little handfuls of it into her mouth. She loved the riotous attention, kicking her legs and screeching.

Around 10:00 p.m., they merrily dropped me off at home. Ma deliberately ignored my entrance, only rolling her eyes when I asked if she got my message, but Dad said that he thinks it's great I met with an old friend who's planning on going back to college. He wants her to sign up for one of his classes.

But now the buzz has died off, and I'm lying in bed, wondering if I'm a person worthy of care or if I lost that right. I touch between my legs to find the tender spot not yet healed.

January 30

I spent the last two days at Dee Dee's. I eat lunch, play with Rae, and get stoned after she goes down for her nap.

They're supposed to move in with Dee Dee's parents tomorrow. The free rent and babysitting will enable Dee Dee to attend college. I told her that moving home is uneventful—a piece of cake. I joked that it's fitting the boys through your window that is trickier than you think. She's still pretty nervous. Seriously procrastinating on the packing.

All she accomplished yesterday was cleaning the bathroom and taking down Rae's crayon drawings. I actually packed most of their clothes into boxes. So cute to see the tiny, pink dresses Rae wore as a newborn. White booties.

Dee Dee gave me several pairs of corduroy overalls that she'd planned to donate to the Goodwill, so I finally own clothes that don't require a thong or a push-up bra. I also located a pair of hiking boots in my closet, allowing me an option besides spiked heels, which I suddenly realize most women in the world do not wear. I feel so short.

Today, in my new attire, I sat in front of Dee Dee's bookcase and packed her books by topic in alphabetical order. Fun to have the absorption, the tunnel-focus that weed gives you, and the warm, heavy physicality that makes small tasks ideal.

Dee Dee zoned out and watched soap operas.

I searched the shelves for more self-help books, running my fingers over shiny spines, until I was momentarily shaken by the snaps of kisses emitting from the television, the noise rushing at me and then pulling away, making me laugh once it seemed more of a game than a threat.

In the evenings, I come home and casually ask Ma if Misty called. She says no and wheedles me to call Sam. I guess we're both used to disappointment.

January 31

Dad lent me his truck to drive to Dee Dee's this morning.

I scrubbed the burners on her stove while she swept. When we finished all the cleaning, I hinted that Rae was cool in her playpen and maybe we could sneak into the bathroom for a smoke.

Distracted, Dee Dee handed me the bag and papers, saying that she didn't want to be fucked up around her parents. Said I could keep the rest. I stammered a thank-you and stood there while she pulled a clean shirt over Rae's head.

Crouching under the bathroom window alone, I took a few drags, feeling pathetic but glad to slip into a haze. My eyes grew dry, and my chest turned warm and heavy. I knew the time to leave them had arrived, so I took out the garbage, gave hugs, and left.

Without thought, I drove to where Rob raped me. I realized that I wanted to make sure I remembered it right.

The only real landmark of the exact spot was a large rock that the front tires of his truck bucked over before we stopped. The tracks of the old road were still there. They ran between two hillsides, brier bushes encroaching on either side.

Snow filled the ditch that I rolled into after he finished. I walked in and out of its dip, comparing the depth to my memory. I'd forgotten about lying there, pressing my hand against the cut on my chest, scared to reach down to hold my vagina, waiting for him to kill me, leave, or put me back in his truck.

I never realized a creek flowed ten or fifteen feet away. The water glowed in the sun. Its cold stung the tips of my fingers as I ran them against the slight current. I was glad he didn't drown me.

Even though I knew, on some level, that the mission was futile, I dug through sections of dirt, looking for any proof, for those sticks I meant to jab in his neck. I collected a handful of sticks that might have been the same ones, though probably not. I ended up throwing them away.

Amazingly, I found a pill bottle stuck in the ground, missing its label and full of red, wet mud. The orange plastic was cracked on one side where someone may have stepped on it or driven over it with their four-wheeler.

Maybe one of us kicked his stash out of the car without noticing. I searched for more but found nothing.

I almost expected the dirt to be dented, or at least bruised, where my body lay while he entered me. But it actually arched up where I found the bottle, toward the sky.

Such a pretty dirt road, lined by pine trees that hiss as they brush against each other in the breeze. I found a crayfish hiding under a rock in the stream, but it slipped away before my eyes could follow. So quiet.

Clenching my hands into fists, I hunched over and screamed and screamed and screamed. Then, silent, I listened for a car to screech to a halt.

But nothing happened. No green-eyed mountain man appeared with a gun to save me. No one showed. Thank god.

Pushing the bottle back into the dirt, I left it there. In case I ever need evidence, I'll lead them to that spot and hope, unrealistically, that he left fingerprints.

From there, I drove to a drugstore and bought brown hair dye.

Ma, excited by the prospect of seeing her natural daughter again, helped me apply the stuff but kept saying, Are you okay? You're looking sick again.

I watched the dirt-colored water swirl in the basin and thought about the creek gliding through the mountains.

With my forehead pressed against the edge of the basin, I began to shake. Ma gripped my shoulders and leaned over, asking me, What's wrong, what's wrong?

Finally I said, I miss New York.

February 1996

February 1

I bought my first car—a used Honda. I'll zip around the country, take dates to drive-in movies, and haunt local drugstores. She's blue with a black, vinyl interior, which is too hot in the summer but easy to clean.

At her suggestion, Ma and I test-drove different cars together. In the one that I eventually bought, we analyzed Sam's girlfriends as I played with the CD player and tested the air conditioner.

Your father is happy that Terri is out of the picture, Ma said.

I swear that no woman is good enough for his son, I said. You both should know Sam isn't exactly a catch.

I lit a cigarette with the car's lighter and blew the smoke out my cracked window, annoying Ma.

Dad's protective is all, she said.

I don't remember him giving my dates a second look.

You didn't let us. In fact, I don't remember any boys from high school except Zach.

That's because there weren't any.

But I thought—

You were wrong, I said and pulled up to the lot's exit.

The clouds waited low and dark down the road, snowflakes dusting the hood. I gunned the engine, flipped on the headlights, and pulled onto the highway.

Ma started touting the benefits of Al-Anon. She said, In the program, they emphasize releasing parental control.

Turning some knob, she accidentally blared classical music under my feet. She wound her wrist back, and the violins retreated.

You see, she continued, an alcoholic must decide to get sober, usually once they hit rock bottom, and my constant worrying, my helping Sam out of trouble, makes me an enabler. She sighed, patting her chest in the comforting, self-congratulating way that drives me crazy.

I grabbed the metal handle next to me and lay my seat back a few inches. Look! I said. I'm cruising like a racecar driver.

She rolled her eyes at me. An eighteen-wheeler tore by, and I jerked at the handle, snapping myself upright.

I agree, she said, that I don't help. He acts hateful when I try.

A gas station sign announced that beer's always on sale.

Ma! I burst out, throwing up one hand. You've gotta learn to be head-on tough instead of passive. Be honest—he respects that. Tell him he's an alcoholic every chance you get. Maybe he'll listen.

You know, I'm happy that you're angry, she said. You have every right. With your dad so calm, and me . . . useless. She reached over and caressed my hair. I brushed her fingers away, saying, Oh, Christ.

Sometimes, she said, I sit at home with no one else around and feel your anger. It's like I'm indulging in a great treat.

I pulled to a stop on a wide shoulder, preparing to U-turn back onto the road.

Find your own anger to play with, I said.

Three cars whipped by, rocking our small car.

I just mean that we need you, she said, almost touching my knee with her hand but pulling back.

I said, I think everyone in this family needs some goddamn self-sufficiency. (Though, even as the words rolled out of my mouth, I didn't believe them.)

Then why are you home? I thought you moved home because you cared.

Of course I care.

Then pay a little attention! Stop getting stoned with your old friends. Help us.

Help you what? I shook my head in bewilderment. Learn to be a happy person? Miraculously cure Sam? What? Exactly what am I supposed to do?

Then she looked confused. I thought you wanted to spend time with me, with your father, she said. I thought you wanted to make that good again.

It was never really good, Ma.

Oh, Tess, she said.

Watching her wipe her nose on her flannel shirt and tuck curls into her bun, I offered this: You look good.

She shot me a half-hearted smile.

The little car felt a bit like home after that.

February 2

While frying potatoes for dinner, Ma updated me on various kids from the neighborhood, informing me that Rob has a job as a computer programmer in Morgantown.

So the fucker lives right by Misty, I thought.

I mumbled that he's a jerk.

Ma stopped flipping potatoes.

Why don't you like him? You never have.

This conversation followed Ma's announcement that she's overlooked me by focusing on Sam recently (for years, I say), and she wants us to catch up. We'll see how long the fad lasts.

Chopping carrots, the juice wetting my fingers, I simply said, Rob bullied people in school. Then I shoved the blade through a thick stem and steered Ma's chatter in a new direction: Now, tell me why you and Dad don't want to move anymore, besides helping Sam.

Oh, she said, the moving had a lot to do with your grandfather. Then, silently, she poured a few drops of vegetable oil into her frying pan. Stirring again, she continued, Once I realized I didn't want to be like him, I slowly let those wandering habits go. But it took a while to realize his flaws. Then changing always takes time. I had to thoroughly wear myself out before I could really settle.

I held still, amazed she admitted that she chose to move, not Dad, and that Sam wasn't the main factor in staying put.

Not wanting to break her mood, I asked cautiously, How did you try to be like Grandpa?

Mostly I just idealized being a nomad, she said, a gypsy. She waved her knife around and shook her head. Your grandfather left us when I was just six months old, you know? Mama and I held no sway over him.

And he never contacted us again, which still shocks me. How could my papa just leave me? The only explanation he gave Mama was that he felt unhappy. He told her this when they kissed goodnight. By the next morning, he had disappeared.

When I was too little to understand the truth, Mama told me that a band of traveling gypsies seduced him. Sometimes she claimed that they placed a spell on him or that his good looks enchanted the group and that they decided to crown him their leader. Their powerful drinks addicted him, she'd tell me as I drifted off to sleep. Their magic potions.

So, of course, I imagined his life—dancing around campfires, playing guitars, sneaking in and out of towns. I thought it sounded magical, even after I noticed the inconsistencies. I read books on gypsies long after she didn't bother softening the truth.

I dreamed of joining my dreamy dad to escape Mama, who reacted to his leaving by clamping down. That woman, may she rest in peace, craved this elusive respectability she had lost when she lost her husband.

And then I grew into a young woman and thought my mother was weak—typical. Compare a woman who gets upset at the sight of poorly washed hands to a man who simply decided to leave because he felt unhappy. Which one looks stronger?

But of course, after you and Sam, I started to realize the hard work in raising kids, keeping together a marriage. And once I tasted those urges to leave, I knew how lazy that choice would be. She shrugged. So, I stopped idealizing my father, and that's why we're still here.

I looked down at my pile of chopped carrots, a bit stunned by her revelations.

Handing me a tomato, she asked, Do you think you might go to the bar with Sam and watch him for a night—see how much he drinks and how he handles it? I'm just being honest about what I want. You can say no.

Further dazed by the sudden shift in gears, I said, I thought Al-Anon said that we shouldn't interfere.

She raised her eyebrows coyly and said, We can still be informed.

I chuckled but didn't give her an answer.

February 3

I attended a therapy session that Ma arranged a while ago.

I liked the therapist. A middle-aged woman—sharp dresser, attractive, not the Earth Mother I dreaded. She said my symptoms and actions were Normal Responses to an Abnormal Experience. She made me describe the rape, tell her about sleeping around. (No need to let everything out of the bag.) I wept buckets, holding onto one destroyed tissue, cringing in a leather chair at my own stories.

Then she said that I'm brave, too brave, which was nice to hear after feeling weak, stupid, and scared for so long.

Staring at the ceiling, she relayed a wonderful and true story. Even if I never see her again, I'll remember the story forever:

A while back, a school bus of children was kidnapped for ransom. The kidnappers drove the bus to a remote area and locked the kids in an underground cavern for approximately twenty-four hours.

During the ordeal, one young boy wanted to help the older ones dig at the rock wall as an attempt at escape. As he tried to help, the older boys pushed him away, ridiculing him for being overweight and useless.

Well, hours went by and eventually the police rescued the children. A psychologist, hearing about the emotional trauma the kids experienced, followed their lives after the event and discovered disturbing patterns, labeled Static Behavior—children repeating the same scenarios over and over.

The littlest kids, still playing in sandboxes, made lines of small creatures climb into a bus and ride a short ways. In the children's hands, the toys slowly walked down the bus steps and filed into a hole in the ground. Then the kids covered the creatures with sand. They played this game endlessly.

In particular, the ridiculed boy reminded the therapist of me. After the kidnapping, he obsessively lost weight and gained strength. Lifted weights for hours every day. As a teenager and young adult, he evolved into a bodybuilder. From there he took on strenuous labor, difficult feats.

He pushed himself and his body until the weight of an object he lifted crushed him to death.

So how many men did I bench-press?

February 4

My mother fantasized about running away from her children. I wonder, Do they all? Probably not. But mine did. And maybe that's not the worst crime you can commit. Anyway, for a kid, I doubt that the allotted attention you receive from your mother is ever enough.

Now we've switched, with good and bad results. I twitch when she lingers in the doorway too long. I can't talk enough for her to stop listening. She wanders into my room and sits on my bed. And she leaves still looking back at me, a bit of yearning left.

I've decided not to resent the late hour of her interest. I'm trying, I suppose, to unstuff myself, to pry my own mouth open. But her attention feels foreign, as if, while she's spreading Vicks ointment onto my chest, her fingers accidentally slip into the tender spot at the base of my neck. I stiffen, nervous.

I visited her in the attic after her Al-Anon meeting today, and she dropped everything. She apologized for pressuring me about Sam.

I saw the brown paint on her temples.

She said, I'm wrong.

You need to relax and keep out of his troubles.

I hushed her and looked at her sketch. Penciled lines, sharp and then smudged. A background of gray branches, delicate and prickly, overlapping. They formed a net or basket. And in the middle were small figures, wispy ashes of me and Sam, half in and half falling through the cracks.

I'm trying something new, she said.

It works, I say.

She's a complex woman trying to hold on. But at least she reaches for us.

February 5

Well, Misty called.

I've been agonizing about our talk, she said. I've been trying to think it out logically. I really need to understand both you and Rob. I know you tend to be honest to a fault, she said, as does Rob. So, in the end, I believe that you didn't want or mean to have sex. Things must've gotten out of hand if you're so upset. My conclusion about Rob is that he must not have understood what was going on with you. He must have been too high to understand. But I'd like you to at least consider forgiving him. He's grown up to be a good guy. Maybe the right thing to do is to give him a chance.

It's my own fault that she's capable of reaching such insane conclusions. I should have called her that night, I thought. I listened to her nice, neat explanation of my rape, and I was heartsick—literally, my heart felt swollen, pushing on my ribs.

Misty changed the subject after her plea for Rob, telling me that she dyed her hair blonde yesterday.

Still too upset to respond to her analysis of me and Rob, I wondered out loud about the timing of her changing hair. Did my revelation make her change? I imagined that the lightness of her new hair eased its weight, and I asked her about this, about being blonde in Morgantown compared to brunette in Elkins.

She sighed.

Before she could answer, I cut in, worried this might be my last chance to ask: Before you leave, before you hang up, tell me—do you remember what I acted like that night? Please. I need to know how I've changed. Please.

She turned quiet, and then she said, You're stranger.

I told her, You're a self-righteous bitch.

I put down the receiver and gave up.

On our porch swing, stoned from Dee Dee's pot, I watch the corner post sliding in and out of my vision. Since the rape, swinging has nauseated me. The sight of potted plants approaching and retreating, my face rushing forward only to be pulled back wears on my innards.

A week ago, a man leaned my head back over the edge of the bed and inserted his penis into my mouth. I let him, pretending I was Linda Lovelace. And today I find that if I carefully pull myself onto a swing and concentrate on relaxing my body, I'll feel a few ripples and then the wood settles—holding me in midair with no sickening sways, just elevation.

Of course, that might just be the marijuana.

I've also arranged a sibling party-night with Sam the day after tomorrow. So we'll count how many beers he drinks. I'll bring a black marker to draw a line over my lips and down my neck for each bottle consumed.

February 6

Drained from crying over Misty, worrying about Sam, trying to accept Ma, and the effort of pushing memories from my mind, I spent the morning in bed and then collapsed onto the couch midafternoon, waiting for Ma's replenishing food.

I found myself suffocating in the heat of the main room, the warmth tenfold above normal because of Ma's insistence on a fire in the fireplace and the stove's output in preparation of a large meal.

Ma hummed in the kitchen and swung her hips to opera, as if arias possess a rhythm. She yelled out the plot to me: This is the scene where women walk out of the cigar factory!

The idea of cigar smoke made me turn green. I remembered kissing a man at the House who tasted like I had stuck my tongue into a can filled with wet, stale cigars.

We heard Dad's truck outside.

The door opened, and our clean, well-dressed men stood in the doorway. Dad kissed Ma on the cheek, giving her a Hmmm . . . of appreciation for the rarely thrown-on blush and perfume.

Sam fell on the couch next to me, wearing shiny, black dress shoes and holding a wrapped present with an obvious outline. A book, I predicted.

Shoot, he said. You're so smart, you could skin a rabbit from the inside out.

He was dead sober. Pale, but dead sober.

What are you two cackling about? Ma yelled.

I shouted back, Do you know how to skin a rabbit from the inside out?

Then Sam pounced, pulling me into a headlock while I tried to yell for help, remembering the Indian kid who pinned me in the House, panic clogging my throat for a moment.

Ma and Dad laughed, and my tension slid onto the floor.

The house pulsed with heat—the air looked pale pink and laughs seemed to send out white ripples.

We ate mashed potatoes that stuck to the roof of my mouth, and I loved it, refusing to think of Rob, refusing to remember potatoes mixed with stomach acid as I vomited onto the dirt road.

Dad joked around at the table. He said, I hate to say this, but some of these kids are so dumb you could fart in one ear, and they'd inhale and blow smoke rings.

He never jokes about his students unless he's high on life.

Sam and I protested against smoker prejudice.

Jesus, woman, Dad said to Ma, could it possibly be any hotter in this house? Why don't you just light the curtains on fire too?

It's just toasty is all!

My feet are actually sweating, Sam said.

It's just fine, Ma said. Isn't it, Tess?

I'm sorry. I can't talk because my tongue has melted into my mouth.

Ma called the feast my pre-birthday party, but the cranberry sauce gliding down my throat definitely tasted like Thanksgiving. When I concentrated, I could almost forget and just see Ma, Dad, Sam, and me sharing a family meal.

Ma insisted that everyone eat two servings of ice cream to bond with the birthday girl in her soft-food diet. I devoured spoonfuls of rocky road, trying to stop sweating, trying to pull away from intrusive, choking memories.

Immediately after dinner, I bolted onto the darkening front porch for a smoke, escaping the heat while the parents did the dishes. Sam grabbed his present as he followed me out.

Open it, he said, letting the screen door slam behind him.

I stuck my cigarette in my mouth and tore at the wrapping. The light from the windows revealed a book on racecar driving and one called *Killing Attackers and Other Means of Self-Defense.*

I laughed at the present and at the relief of the cold air seeping into my warm clothes.

Sam said, I figured this way you'll be fine while I'm in jail. You won't even think to rely on me, you'll be so tough. He lit his cigarette.

Thanks, I said and took a final drag on my own cigarette, dropping it into the can of water Ma stuck on the porch for me. I hopped into the yard and grabbed a handful of snow.

Hey! he said.

What? I'm just eating some snow. Cools me down.

He turned to look in the window, when . . . BAM, I splattered him on his forehead. I hooted because a perfect shot only comes once a year.

The coolness of my hands woke me, melted the numbing warmth.

And soon Ma, Dad, and Sam stood on the porch, yelling at me to come in from the cold and dark, that I was gonna freeze to death. I packed more cannonballs of snow and bombed 'em one at a time. I hit Ma on her chest; Dad, on the side of his head. My hair swung up and down as I dipped for more, reveling in my body and its strength as I pulled back my shoulders, extended, and flipped my wrist like Sam taught me when I was nine so I could help him beat the neighborhood crew in battles; for a while there, we always won.

I jogged around the yard, taunting Sam. I slapped him in the middle of his crotch with a big, sloppy one.

He dove off the porch, grabbing handfuls and pelting me. Ma chased him, shouting at him to leave his sister alone.

Tripping backward, I fell and saw gray tree branches resting against the moon.

Then I leapt to my feet and started singing, She's a maniac, maniac on the floor. (I hit Ma on her leg, swooping down for more as Ma slid and fell over.) Dancing like she's never danced before! I squatted over my mother, and, with my cupped hands, I was shoveling snow up her shirt until, with no warning, Sam loomed over me and dumped an armful of snow on my head, pouring it down in chunks over my flushed face, the snow puffing on my shoulders and legs, bursting next to Ma. Dad applauded in the distance.

Sound filled my ears as I continued to sing, holding a long, hard note that should have cued the magician to snap the curtain off the cage, and what was meant to disappear would be gone, and left behind would be Ma, Sam, and me playing in the snow and Dad cheering us from the porch. And that would be all.

February 8

It's five o'clock in the morning. The sky is dark, and no one else is awake. I made myself some tea before finding my way to this page.

Last night, I met Sam outside of his place. As I pulled up beside him, he ground out his cigarette and opened the door of my car.

I wanted to see your place, I said.

Later, he said, sliding in and rubbing his whole face with his hand as if he'd woken minutes before.

But you've become a famous wall-artist, I said.

I'll let you see it later. He slapped the dashboard and said, Let's go. I need a drink.

Hurt, I pulled onto the road but avoided his trash this time.

Not speaking, we drove to his favorite watering hole about fifteen minutes away.

The Shop is crammed between a barbershop and diner. You open a glass door on street level and walk down red-carpeted stairs to a smallish room packed with men and women leaning on each other, hanging onto a horseshoe-shaped bar.

The bartender, an old guy with a ponytail, called out, Sammy! How ya been? Hey, who's the pretty lady?

Sam leaned back and boomed out a laugh that sounded more like a cry of relief. Ha! Ha! You watch your mouth, Dean; this is my kid sister.

We walked up, and a space cleared as women nodded and a few guys slapped Sam on the back. I was in *Cheers: The Alcoholic Version*—the pilot episode that hit too close to home.

Sorry about that, Dean said, smiling at me. I've never seen this guy with a respectable woman is all. Yes, I can see the resemblance. Dark ones, the both of you. What can I do you for?

Sam slipped off his coat. Give me a fishbowl of Bud, and Tess will have . . . ? He turned toward me, but his eyes scanned the crowd.

A screwdriver sounds good, I said. Dean winked, and Sam walked across the room to talk to a man and woman upholstered in blue jean, shirt to sock.

Dean placed a huge goblet full of beer on the counter.

Hey, I lifted my chin to point. What's that?

A fishbowl, Dean said. Holds about two pints for our boy. He pulled orange juice out of his mini-fridge.

The crowd was a mix of old alcoholics and young college bingers listening to country music on the jukebox. Sam took a long drink from one of his friend's glasses, a man with a goatee. Garth Brooks's voice swung into the room through the speakers.

I got friends in LOW places, where the whiskey drowns and the beer chases my blues away, Garth sang. Everyone joined in. Sam stomped his foot and sang along. He even did a few line-dancing steps with Mr. Goatee's blonde date. My brother was beautiful in the bar. The low lights made his face appear slimmer, more handsome.

The last time I remembered seeing him this exuberant, he'd just turned thirteen and danced through the house in his new cowboy boots and red swimming trunks, jumping on the couch, pretending to be a rock star—Elvis singing "Hound Dog."

The song finished, and Sam joined me, grabbing his fishbowl and pointing to a table on the other side of the room.

Who's the guy with the goatee?

Oh, Mick runs Dino's . . . you know, the restaurant where I work.

Oh, right, I said.

Don't worry. I never remember the places you work either.

You're not supposed to, I said, watching him take a drink. I wondered how to calculate his beer consumption when I didn't understand how much one glass held. I pointed to some of his apparent friends. Why don't you introduce me?

He waved his hand in front of his face. You don't want to meet them, he said, adding, They're not good with women.

Well, how about some of the other people you said hi to?

This is a rough crowd.

I stared at him. Listen, old-timer, you think I haven't seen rougher in New York?

Yeah, well. You're with your big brother right now.

Fine, I said, refusing to fluster so early in the evening and annoyed because he wanted to fit in with this crowd, wanted acceptance as a local country boy, but was also embarrassed by those who argued about the latest guests on Jerry Springer. He didn't believe that they'd like me.

Maybe because I've traveled more, I tend to have unquestioning loyalty to any fellow West Virginian. I say that the state benefits from the politics of the hippies and from the strength of the laborers. We're bonded by mountains, rivers, and obnoxious stereotypes.

A couple more hours passed with us shooting the shit about how many generations we'd have to live in West Virginia to be considered natives, adjusting to home, and his hopes of winning the lottery (which I mocked him for). He said that if he doesn't hit the jackpot within the next year, after jail he plans on heading to Florida to bartend. I want a life of leisure, he said.

His eyes continued to scan the crowd, and occasionally I'd give him permission to jump up and do a few fake punches in a friend's gut, and then return.

By his fourth fishbowl, his hands and head flopped. Both of us chain-smoked.

Johnny Cash growled out of the jukebox, and Sam seemed to forget about his latest cigarette. He let it burn until an inch of ash hung on for dear life.

I reached over and tapped his finger to shake it off.

Hey, watch it! he said, smacking my hand away, hurting my fingers.

My temper flared. I was knocking your ash off is all!

Oh, he said.

Listen, you're wasted. In fact, you're so drunk, it's making me nervous. So, let's go.

What? He squinted his eyes.

I leaned back from the table and said, I want you to stop drinking and leave with me.

You're the one who wanted to go out. He pointed a finger toward me. All you gotta do is drive me home. We'll leave in a half hour.

I stared at the ashtray. Butts stuck up like the stems of plucked flowers.

He reached for another sip.

I leaned close and whispered, Don't you take another fucking drink or I will leave your ass here to rot.

He reared back, almost sliding sideways off his chair. Christ, Tess! Just let me finish my drink. I'm not hurting anybody.

No, I said.

Come on! He defiantly took a gulp of beer and looked away.

You're full of shit, Sam. Such bullshit.

No I'm not, he said and blinked his welling eyes, pulling another cigarette out of the pack.

Your drinking doesn't hurt people?

He held his cigarette between his fingers and poked at the table. I'm sorry I didn't drive you that night. How could I have known? Huh? I'm sorry, I'm sorry, I'm sorry, I'm sorry. What else can I do? I gave you those books. Do you want my soul?

I want you to learn. How sorry do you have to be before you stop?

That little boy got over it, he said. His parents dropped the case. Everybody is okay now. They're all right. I called and made sure.

You want praise? You want me to say how great it is that you called them—let's all have a drink and a cheer for Sam? How about this instead? I stared at him, and he looked at his beer. I said, Your magic potion won't save you tonight.

Moonshine, I began, at Fiser's farm. You were hypnotized. You didn't feel me tapping you on the shoulder, shivering from the wind, you were so entranced.

A tear slid down into his mustache, over his lips.

Me asking for a simple favor. Me saying that you could come back and hang out more later. But you didn't want to miss out on the yum-yum moonshine. I hitched a ride, and I was raped.

Obviously, Sam, you took note of this, but even now you still ask me to stamp it out of my gut. No! Terror every time I'm alone with a guy. Every goddamn time. My skin crawls even when you or Dad touches me.I found myself jabbing my finger at the table. When my fingertip slid against his cold fingers, I jerked away.

Of course, the story gets worse, I continued. Sitting in the middle of New York, I said to myself, Face it. I will never love, never move on, until I beat this fear out of me. I will face it head on, not like you, the way you sink into oblivion. So, I started screwing for money. The more experience, the better, I figured. The more fear I'd deal with, the more I'd control it. But guess what? My theory didn't work. I just got hurt over and over. Scared over and over. I've learned my fucking lesson. But here you are, the same person no matter how many mistakes you make.

He lifted up his palm and hit himself on the side of the head.

Your guilt does not cut it! I was sliced and beat and torn apart.

I sucked in air and pressed my eyes with a cocktail napkin, pressing away tears.

Sam leaned his head between his forearms.

You were supposed to take care of me, I said. Why did you stop—ever? Why didn't you stick with me?

And I remembered him wandering into the house throughout high school with a smirk on his face and his body heavy with alcohol.

When he didn't answer, I grabbed my purse and ran. The cold pushed me back a step as I pulled open the door, but I ducked down and ran to my car.

Figuring that Sam wasn't capable of doing much damage to himself without a car, and that Dean would probably make him sleep there, I roared home, crawled onto my futon, and slept for a couple of hours.

I'll call Sam when the sun has risen, to make sure he's all right. I hope we're okay. I don't know.

Later in the evening: I'm scared because I can only reach Sam's answering machine. I called Sue at her new temp job this afternoon.

I recited the gist of the conversation, and she decided that I spoke honestly at first, harshly at the end.

I turned him into my scapegoat. I'm such an asshole. Jesus.

No words of advice from Sue—only that she's sorry and loves me. She asked how she could help. I said I didn't know.

I can't believe I blamed him for my entire life. As if I had no choice in the matter. As if he's obliged to be my guardian forever. Shit, shit, shit.

February 9

Sam painted ROB IS A RAPIST on the front of Rob's home. He added a simple RAPIST on each side—five-foot-tall, red letters.

I'm relieved he's alive.

Ma drove us past the house on the way to the grocery store. Sloppy and lopsided, the letters are still clear. I slouched down as we cruised by, wondering what was going on inside. Ma heard that the police don't want to paint over the writing until they examine the evidence further.

Imagine the drama. Heated denials, I suppose, or lukewarm. Maybe Misty and Rob are whispering on the phone and think I wrote the accusation. Maybe there will be enough fear from now on that Sam's risk will have been worth it.

Ma asked me if I thought Rob could be a rapist—after all, I don't like him.

I shrugged and said I wouldn't be surprised.

Really?

Wouldn't be surprised At All.

She shook her head as she turned the car into our driveway.

My brother is a goofball. And I want to sing about him to the world, sing his adventures. My painting defender!

Also, Ma's frantic since the message on Sam's machine now says that he left town to visit friends. The court hearing is less than a month away, and he's screwed if he doesn't show.

We called all the local bars, but no luck.

Dad found out that Dean did give him a ride home.

I guess that after he left the bar, he passed out until the next evening. He woke with a pounding head. Then, I imagine, he sat around brooding.

Anger pushing in on him, he headed out with a can of paint and a brush hidden in a paper bag or under his coat. Maybe he hitchhiked, but more likely he biked the fifteen miles to Rob's house, hiding in the bushes until every light went dark. He knelt down, remembering the bathroom, me.

Clenching his jaw, he crept toward the house, dipping his brush into the can of paint, beginning with an *R* on the side of the house in case a car drove by. Dead sober, or maybe not, he quietly stroked the wood, just wanting people to know, hoping another girl might come forward because of the sign and the town would lynch Rob, beat him to death.

Sweaty and tired, he finished and ran to the highway. He threw the can into the dumpster behind the Jiffy Mart. And, careful no paint had splattered his clothes, he hitchhiked to a friend's to wait out the storm.

I can't help rolling my eyes at his idealism, his imagination. What a sweet, sweet guy. I'm actually proud, smiling because he's my brother and I'm his sister.

February 10

Over breakfast, Ma jabbered about church gossip and then said, You know, Sam disappeared on the same night that Rob's house was painted. I keep wondering if they're connected. Maybe something happened with one of Sam's girlfriends.

Ma!

Well, where is he? Where did he go? He's never left like this. We should tell the police.

He's visiting friends, I said.

Yeah, but what friends? I called his friends all over the country, and no one has seen him. She rubbed hard at the oil paint on her hands.

Don't call the police, I said, but she didn't pay attention. I threw up my hands. He left because we fought! I yelled. All right? We went to the bar and fought. He'll come back. You don't need to call anybody.

I refused to reveal what we'd fought about. I'm too awful—not for the hooking or stripping (those were just blows to me) but for blaming Sam . . . unacceptable. Ultimately, I am responsible for my own life. And Rob is responsible for the rape.

Ma wanted to know if the fight was connected to the painted accusation.

I wouldn't answer, only repeated that Sam would come back.

Resting her head on her arms, she cried and didn't ask me any more questions.

Stepping outside, I sat on the porch swing. Pandy meowed at the door, but I sat still and elevated even as the cold wind lifted my hair. Big snowflakes flew through our countryside this afternoon. Big as stars.

February 11

Ma tattled to Dad that I fought with Sam, wanting him to pressure the truth out of me.

Dad said, You need to talk in order to help your brother. You may contain useful information. Stuff you don't even realize. (You'd think he was Mr. Private Eye and Sam hid a secret chip in my brain.)

So, the long and short of it is: I wouldn't spill the beans, and now Dad won't speak or look at me until I do.

I'm scared. I don't want a trial. I don't want them to be angry with Sam. He did his best.

Please, please let me know he's all right. Please, don't hurt yourself, Sam. Hop back on a bus, and let's settle something for once. We'll keep calm and talk on the swing.

Ma makes me nervous and sad to watch. I avoid her. And then she tracks me down to hand me cup after cup of tea. I guess she's figured out that I'm the Raped Girl. But I shouldn't care that she finally understands me and my pain. I should concentrate on Sam, though I thank god that Ma's sad and not angry.

But before Ma blurted out her suspicion, I slipped away to Dad's shop and sat amongst the half-built harps. Bored, I dug through stacks of materials and found the Hiding Box that Dad made for me long ago. The edges were as smooth as I remembered.

The smell of mothballs made me sneeze as I climbed in and closed the lid. I felt claustrophobic and wondered for the first time whether Dad should have made a box for his little girl who needed to talk. Then I killed some time pulling out the nails with a hammer and dismantling the entire piece.

Sam. You liked working in his shops. You probably don't remember the one Christmas when you and I had nothing to do because the wind knocked trees onto our power lines. We spent the day making snow angels and drawing top hats for the winged creatures to tip. You said that we should design cutting boards, and how if the power came back, we'd sneak down and saw them in Dad's shop. You said that you missed that place after Dad kicked you out.

I pretended that I didn't hear you because I was shocked to realize that Dad had lied about the incident by focusing on your Acting Out. In his version, you hated the work.

But I never said a word. I never made Dad apologize. I never even grunted or rolled my eyes at parties when he described Sam's Teenage Antics.

February 12

Because Sam still hasn't called, I drove to his place to see if he's hiding. No sign of him. I slipped a knife in the door crack, pushing the latch back.

Towers of beer bottles stood pressed so tight against the ceiling that the structure curved in the middle.

He'd taken the paint set that Ma gave him for Christmas and painted caricatures of our family on his kitchen walls. There was fresh paint partially erasing my fictional nose piercing. My hair was painted back to its natural brown, though the heavy frown was not gone and he hadn't softened the razor angles of my face. Next was one of Dad smashing a cutting board over his own head.

With her own wall, Ma was a foot taller than the rest of us. It was a side view of her stomping though a field of flowers, dead grass and browned flowers appearing where she had already stepped, arms swinging by her side, her hair streaming behind her.

Christ, no wonder he never let us visit. Scathing, opinionated prick. Makes me laugh. I don't give a shit. Everyone would faint if they read this journal. All that matters is that I don't have a clue where he's gone. His bike is missing, so he probably dumped it on his way out, the wheels spinning in the breeze across from Rob's house.

Back home, I walked into the woods and pulled myself onto the lowest branch of a tree. The view sloped down our hill, stopped by the tree-lined road and the raised forest beyond. Smoke rose from our chimney. My back pressed against the rough bark. Fidgeting like a five-year-old who needs to use the bathroom, I concluded that doing nothing accomplishes nothing.

So now I'm in front of the family computer. I need to write a letter for my parents, describing the rape and events following (omitting the brothel for now).

I'll start off talking about the kidnapped kids the therapist described. I'm not some freak of nature after all, and I refuse to lose more friends or family through blowups and silences.

February 13

I received a letter from Sam. My name was typed on an envelope with no return address, so Ma and Dad don't know that he wrote me. He's in Lewisburg. Though he didn't say so, the postmark gave him away. The only thing he wrote was a page of apologies, literally—I'm sorry, I'm sorry, I'm sorry, I'm sorry—filling the entire piece of paper, making me cry. I'm terrified it's a suicide note, but I can't believe he would do that. He has never managed to leave us.

In fact, none of us knows how to walk away. I also failed in that regard. It's probably our family's greatest strength as well as its greatest weakness—our undying sense of connection. A bunch of goddamn codependents.

In the psych class at NYU, we read that the Nazis performed experiments by placing babies in bare rooms with minimal contact. They fed and cleaned them but shared no communication or real touch. The children simply died. Some grew mentally retarded and then died. The babies couldn't develop.

We label fear and anger as the primitive emotions, sex and aggression the primitive drives, but the desire to communicate . . . it's an absolute necessity in our ability to survive. The desire to connect burns in our first breath. We embrace that need from the moment a nurse scoops the gunk out of our mouths.

I can't fight that need to connect with the ones I love anymore. I must believe the desire still burns in Sam.

February 14

Ma and Dad received my letter, which included the fact that Sam wrote to me. I handed them two copies after dinner last night, said that I'd be back in an hour, and went to my room. Lying on my bed, I turned up the radio to block out the sounds of shouts or cries. I hummed to the music and held Sam's letter.

My alarm went off, and I walked back into the living room.

Ma sat in front of the fire. Dad was gone.

I took a breath and decided not to be angry with him because regaining my family means I've survived it all. It's my triumph. It's my Fuck You! to Rob.

Ma pulled me into her arms, saying, We're so sorry for accusing you of drinking. Awful parents, awful.

She rocked with me on the couch and stroked my hair so hard that she hurt my head.

I apologized for being so angry with her. I should have told you, I said.

She said that Dad wants to call the cops.

I smiled and said that wasn't necessary—or desired—as I wiped my tears.

I figured that you'd want to forget it, said Ma.

No I don't, I said. Ma, I'm not into your whole denial thing. I never want to see him again, but I don't want to forget.

I closed my eyes and imagined shouting to the world—I WAS RAPED!

Sliding off Ma's lap, I said, I expected psychic powers to inform you that Rob raped me. Unreasonable, I know. And Sam didn't give me a ride the night it happened. I've sort of wanted to kill him for years because of it. I screamed at him in the bar, told him that he's been a horrible brother, that his drinking had basically caused the rape.

Yes, yes, Ma said, hugging me to her again.

But it's not Sam's fault anymore, I said. Rob is the rapist. Rob is the rapist, right?

Right, Ma said.

She's overwhelmed, so I'm letting her be. I apologized again for not saying anything earlier, for blaming too many people.

I'm picturing Sam hungry, drunk, and freezing in the high mountains around Lewisburg—thinking he's worthless, responsible for my life. Maybe I'll go after him. I might take off and bring him home. Convince him that I've punished him and myself enough.

It's Valentine's Day, and I'm twenty-one years old.

February 15

Pandy is asleep on our bed in a hotel room just outside of Lewisburg.

This morning, before I left the house, my day-after-birthday break-fast became divine when Sue called, pulling me away from my stunned parents, sounding healthy and strong. She's bitch-slapped her new roommate into shape and is actually learning to like the girl.

Most impressive, she's applied to various acting programs, including Carnegie Mellon in Pittsburgh, which would bring her back into my part of the world!

I talked about Sam, wondering if his lawyer might be able to argue for house arrest and if his money is running out. I talked until I said, Never mind! I'm gonna find him. I'm going to Lewisburg!

You go on with your bad self! Sue said.

And I threw open my closets. Ready to hit the road within thirty minutes, I stood by the door and said my goodbyes. I kissed Dad's cheek and stroked his jaw, regretting the shadows under his eyes.

Ma insisted on walking me out, fluttering around my car until I put my arm around her shoulders and headed a short ways down the road. Pandy ran out in front, batting at pieces of gravel, her tail high as she leapt. We stopped on the bridge, watching the water snake into the culvert.

Ma, I said, when I get back, I'm gonna look for a job and my own place. I'll go back to school, and maybe Sam can live with me. Give you two a break.

Ma laughed and said, Slow down, Wonder Woman. You might want some help healing too. Why don't you focus on finding Sam first? But, Tess, if he refuses to be found, please just come home. Or if he's just gone, for whatever reason, make sure to come home.

I promised to come back soon.

In the meantime . . . , she said, her voice trailing off.

Watch for a call from Western Union, I quipped.

Giggles and tears. We hugged. And on a whim, we prodded each other to climb down the bank to the mouth of the culvert.

Swinging ourselves in, we braced our feet on either side of the arching metal walls.

We stuck our hands out, fingertips grazing the cool sides for balance, scooting each foot forward, watching the waves lick at the edges of our boots.

Boo, I yelled, and it echoed right back. The tunnel filled with my voice and the rushing black water under us. Our bodies spread wide like spiderwebs. Dim light peered in the ends, casting our shadows. Water gushed up the indented ripples of the walls, protecting us like the rib cage of a whale.

Ma yelped, Aieee, and pounded her foot.

I joined her, booing and ooh-ing in the blackness, laughing and screeching. The noise cocooned us in its curves. We stood tall in the eye of the storm we created.

So I've decided to end this journal. To put aside my last hideaway.

My hand moves smoothly now, sweeps deeper into the page.

I want that truth to be how I weave through my waking life.

In order to keep *Surviving Mae West* tightly focused on the complex individuality of Tess and her life, I chose not to analyze certain components of her reaction to the rape (such as her compulsive desire to repeat the destructive scenario and her intrusive thoughts). The narrative, however, was predicated on the idea that Tess is suffering from Post-Traumatic Stress Disorder (PTSD), a condition that can be significantly helped with therapeutic treatment.

ABOUT THE AUTHOR

Priscilla Rodd was born outside Paw Paw, West Virginia, in an old farmhouse without running water or electricity. Her birth was overseen by a midwife who was paid fifty dollars and three old chickens for her services. Her parents, Quaker activists, home-schooled Priscilla until she was eleven years old. She began public school the same year her family acquired indoor plumbing and a black-and-white television. Priscilla holds an M.F.A in fiction from the University of Pittsburgh. She currently teaches creative writing and lives in Charles Town, West Virginia, with her husband and fellow writer, Deane Kern, and their two young sons.